A SOMETHING LIKE LOVE SERIES NOVEL

I Like You, I Love Her

BESTSELLING AUTHOR OF LA DOULEUR EXQUISE

J. R. ROGUE

This is a work of fiction. Names, characters, places, and incidents are a product of the author's imagination. Locales and public names are sometimes used for atmospheric purposes. Any resemblance to actual people, living or dead, or to businesses, companies, events, institutions, or locales
is completely coincidental.

Edited by Christina Hart
Proofread by Julie Deaton
Cover art by Pink Ink Designs
Print and E-Book interior design by J.R. Rogue

J.R. Rogue
PO Box 984
Lebanon, MO 65536
www.jrrogue.com
contact@jrrogue.com

CONTENTS

For Désirée, Akia, Erica, Brenda, & Holly

We didn't listen to the rules. We made our own for a moment. High school would have been unbearable without you.

TOTO

YOU CAN GO HOME—THE SAYING IS WRONG—THOUGH IT'S
rarely under the circumstances you would hope for.

"Looks like we aren't in California anymore," I mutter to my
passenger as I drive past the Burlingame Kansas city limit sign,
squinting my eyes at wildflowers and fields shorn, yellow like the
summer heat. When I roll under the bridge right before one can
catch sight of the cobblestone road, I know there's no turning back.

When you escape a town like this for something bigger, you never
want to return. But life rarely listens to your plans.
Sometimes *you* don't even listen to your plans.

Driving my little Volkswagen Beetle back home wasn't practical. I
could have flown and picked up a car in Topeka, but I wanted to see
the country. To draw this out. And maybe, to avoid things for as
long as I could. I hate to admit it, but I'm very good at that. It's a
skill I wish I didn't have.

I look at my passenger, staring out the window, drool collecting on the glass. "We're here, Toto." I laugh to myself, but my dog, Beau, doesn't get the joke.

He stares back at me, with big brown eyes and a lopsided grin. He was an excellent riding companion, something I worried about. The farthest I had taken my German Shepherd before this was a two-hour trip out of town and jumping into this one was pushing it. But leaving my best friend home wasn't an option I would even consider.

Now, I could proudly say, we had crossed states together.

It's seven a.m. on a Monday now, and I didn't think I would be eager to see my old town, but I am.

I wanted to arrive the night before, but I had been pushing myself, as usual, to hit an impossible deadline.

My eyes were tired, and the coffee I drank for dinner wasn't helping. So, we made one last motel stop off I-70 and called it a night. I wanted to clear my head before I had to face the reality of our father's situation. I wanted to lie in bed with my notebook, document this feeling. All I ended up doing was drawing a shitty sketch of an ominous figure and a teenage girl I couldn't bring myself to think of. I couldn't bring myself to name or remember a few other things, either. But avoiding them here would be impossible.

The grim reaper had been staring over my shoulder my entire life. His presence was always heavy. My father was forty-two when I was born. My mother, thirty-six. I was young when we lost her. My memories of her are faded, and they mostly spring from old photos, rarely from my mind. I also find her in stories my older sister Sasha tells me. My father rarely brought her up, but when we asked questions, he would answer.

When I was little, I wanted to know everything I could. As I got older, I saw the way my constant need for him to relive their life together wounded him. The way his eyes turned sad around the edges as the stories fell out.

For me, she was an image, my birthplace, a riddle I couldn't quite figure out. For him, she was a wound. One I kept opening without care, without thought because I didn't know. She was a fairytale princess, a home I would never visit again. More idea than woman.

I was three when she left us.

She never left him. Never let him move on.

The little girl in me hoped that if I stopped asking about her, he would move on, remarry. But he never did. It was a hope of my sister's, one instilled in me by her, something I carried on.

And my father, he said he was content. He liked to drive his school bus, and he walked our dogs. He took Sasha and me to the mall, a half hour away in Topeka, on Saturdays. Because, like most girls, we loved to shop. To dress up and play make-believe. With the age gap, I was playing make-believe in my bedroom, pretending to be the characters in the stories I read. My sister was playing make-believe at school. Pretending to be the girl the boys wanted. Pretending to want the boys in return.

On Sundays, my father took us to church. We learned about God from Pastor Winthrop. When we came home, I assembled puzzles with my father on the dining room table. My sister worked on her homework, watched TV, and talked on the phone with her friends for hours.

When I told my father I wanted to move to New York, following in my sister's footsteps, leaving him alone, he didn't hesitate to support me.

He promised to visit, to leave anchoring, stifling Kansas for us. And he did. Every summer.

When I moved to LA, he promised to visit me there, too, wanting to see the West Coast beaches again, where he once lived before he was a father. When he wasn't coming to me or Sasha, he was meeting us in the middle. Vacations to the mountains in Colorado. Vacations to The Rockies.

Time is a strong and strange thief. His health started to fail. My phone calls home confirmed what I dreaded, what I feared most.

He was losing his memories, his mind, the most sacred pieces of him—the well of understanding and knowledge my sister and I always came to when we feared the world, or ourselves.

Sasha came home when she could since she was a freelance web designer and could work anywhere, but I never found the time except once, when I spent a few days in Topeka where my father was in the hospital. But I never came to Burlingame again. I wanted to avoid the problem. I wanted to avoid my home and the way it took and took and took from me. If I pretended it didn't exist, maybe it wouldn't.

I was wrong. I can see it now. When I pull onto the main street, I blow out a breath.

It's a time warp. Towns like this seem to be stuck in glass jars. I want to grab this one, shake it up.

The road below me is cobblestone, and my little car rumbles, jostling me in my seat. I throw my loose arm over my breasts. *Fuck, I should have worn a bra.*

The buildings I pass, my speed now dropped to twenty mph, are brick, old. They painted new buildings in bright colors, setting them apart. I pass the post office, the city hall, Harold's Hardware, Betty's Bakery. The Falcon's Nest.

I stop looking around, stare ahead. "Focus," I say, and Beau glances at me. My chest aches and my mind turns over images of the picnic table sitting outside The Falcon's Nest. It's still there. I wonder if my name is still carved on the seat.

Will I see someone I know soon? Will they know I'm here? Can I just hide away?

The town is busy. It's the last week of school, and I see two yellow buses on surrounding streets.

A cluster of farmers sits outside Lazy Lee's gas station, coffee in hand, shooting the breeze.

I feel sixteen again, and I'm not sure how I feel about that.

I roll down Beau's window a little more, and he sticks his head out as far as he can, inhaling every scent Burlingame offers.

No sooner am I on the main street that I'm off, turning left down the road that leads to my old house.

In LA, it takes you over an hour to get anywhere in the city.

In Kansas, an hour's drive will take you through a handful of towns.

It's easier to escape.

When I pull into the driveway, my eyes immediately fly to my rearview mirror.

The old high school doesn't look the same. Construction trucks sit on the front lawn. The old red brick building is a shadow in my mind. My eyes travel up the three-story building, and a million stories scramble in my mind to be the first one I replay.

Too many memories, too many heartbreaks.

My Aunt Vera walks out onto my old front porch, pulling my eyes forward. I grab the key from the ignition and step out into the hot Kansas heat. I hold the door open long enough for Beau to jump across the center console. He immediately finds my old mailbox and takes a piss.

"Severin! My darling girl," my aunt hollers.

I roll my eyes at my dog and laugh, pointing at him as he finds a new spot to circle and take a shit. *Fuck, I'm going to step in that later.* I can just see it.

"Aunt V!" I turn to her and slam the door, then bounce up the steps. She catches me in her arms. She smells of pancakes, maple syrup, the past. I release my aunt and turn back to the trucks for a moment, shaking my head. I feel like I'm hallucinating.

"I've missed you so much," I say. The last time I saw her I was a senior in high school. I was a child, ready to see the world, not ready for the heartbreak I would experience before I left. Not ready for the way my world would end before it even began.

"You, too. It's been too long since you came home."

I try not to flinch at her words. At the guilt churning there. I avoid her eyes, turn around. "What's going on with the high school?" My hands go to my hips, my eyes become tiny little slits. The Kansas sky is blue and blinding and I need to be sure I'm seeing what I think I'm seeing.

"They built a new one. Just outside of town, to the east. Your father didn't tell you that? It was about five years ago."

"No." I narrow my eyes at the red brick building. I need my glasses. My father talked little about the school anymore. Not since he stopped driving his bus, closing that chapter of his life. I'm not surprised they built a new one. I remember the failing window air units my senior year. The outdated facility was pushing it even then.

"How old was that building, anyway?"

"Over a hundred years old, I think?" She places a hand on my shoulder, and I lean into her, my cheek resting there. "I reckon you could say it was time."

"What are they doing with it?"

"Oh, someone bought it, I hear. The city auctioned it off on the courthouse steps. It's being turned into low-income apartments."

"Isn't everyone here low income?" I step away, softening my face when I look at my aunt again. I'm not trying to jab, it's just a truth. You move to a place like Burlingame because it's quiet, cheap. Topeka is a half hour away, so you have the city's convenience close by.

"Low income for women looking to start over." My aunt's voice is soft and soothing. I remember the way it sounded on the other line of the phone when I was a little girl. I would call her when my father grounded me. I begged her to reason with him. She would laugh and ask me what I did wrong. When our mistakes and sins are repeated from our own mouths, we often see ourselves in a new light.

I look at her hard. Her eyes are the same blue as my father's.

One night, years ago, she came to our house to stay. I overheard her talking to my father, her twin, in the living room, while I was supposed to be asleep. I pressed my little ear to the carpet and watched their feet from beneath my door in the small crack of light.

Her husband had hit her. Blackened her eye, gripped her arms and left violent and green marks there, slowly fading to yellow. I never spoke of it, the things I wasn't old enough to know, but I clutched her tightly the next day. She stayed the whole summer with us, getting back on her feet. That was the summer I pretended I had a mother.

The sound of car doors slamming pulls me from my memory. I grab my aunt's hand and squeeze it.

"You hungry? I made pancakes and eggs for your father. The food at the home isn't nearly as good as what I can make. So I take him what I can."

"Yeah, I'll be in soon. I'm just going to grab a few things."

"Okay, darling, I'm in your sister's old room, so your old room is free. You'll be sharing with Sasha when she gets in, or one of you can set up that tent in the den. You're picking her up from the airport, right?"

"Yes. She gets in tomorrow afternoon." I need her. My lifeline. I feel so close to her, even when she's miles away. I wonder if it was like that for my father and my aunt. If the twin connection was so strong they could feel each other's pain no matter where they were. Can she feel his pain now?

I walk back to my car, popping my trunk and reaching for my hair tie on my wrist. It's already too hot. I gather my sandy locks at the nape, pull them up.

A man walking across the lawn of the old high school catches my eye just as I secure my messy bun. I watch him walk to a pickup, the one that caught my eye earlier. I study his gait as he reaches the tailgate, letting it fall.

My breath stops, my cheeks flush.

Fuck. I didn't expect to see him, the first boy I loved, so soon.

HIJACK HOMECOMING

PAST

His fingers were long, delicate almost. I wrote poetry about them, late at night, long past my bedtime under a dim lamp.

I watched the other students, brows furrowed, answering essay questions in a hurry. Time was slipping away. Their teacher was gone, but they did not act out in her presence.

I was always more lenient on them, since they were my peers, and I didn't want to make enemies. No one wants enemies in high school. And I didn't want my crush, Bryan Winthrop, Pastor Winthrop's son, to think I was more of a square than he surely did already.

I pulled my eyes from his hands and focused back on my desk, pressed against Mrs. Michaels'. I was doodling. A small snail stared back at me with oval cartoon eyes. I looked at my own hands. Long and delicate fingers, just like his. Piano hands. I wondered what they would look like interlocked, threaded.

There was rain pelting the open windows that day. The hot September air had cooled, and the second period English class begged their teacher to open the windows.

The light inside the classroom was a shade or two brighter than the sky outside.

When it happened, I thought perhaps it was static in the air. My hair rose at the back of my neck, so I reached back, rubbing the area. I looked over my shoulder, trying to find the window again, but my eyes caught on Bryan.

He was staring at me, his pencil dangling from his lips. I knew he wasn't done with his test. I had helped grade his papers and though I hated to admit it, my crush was not at the top of the class.

I blushed at the smile sitting at the corner of his mouth.

I wanted to mouth 'what?' or do something. But I always froze. I knew he liked that about me. He toyed with my reactions, the color of my skin. And I marched on, slowly, like I'd been wound up by his delicate fingers, though they'd never touched my own burning flesh.

But really it was those stares that kept my crush going, that fueled me. These heated, locked-in moments were all I had. They were between us alone, and I knew they would never step over the edge, free fall into something more profound.

Social status denied us that. We were slaves to high school hierarchy. Well, he was a slave to it. I didn't care.

I broke the connection with him then, suddenly, a little angry. I stared at my hands and the trembling there. I clenched my fists to steady myself.

How could a teenage boy hold such arrogance? Such power over another? It should be illegal.

I was so easily pliable, pushed to a reaction. My friends said they loved that about me. They loved my firecracker ways. I didn't have Bryan's restraint, his ability to pull a smile, a blush, from someone. I reacted to him. I never made moves of my own. I never tested my power, because I knew, with him, I had none.

I knew this truth—reminded myself of it daily—because if I had that power he wielded so carelessly, I would have used it on him already. It had been two years of this torturous crush, and I needed a release. One he could give me, or a self-given freedom from this attraction.

He wasn't always this person in front of me, with this ability to pull something, anything from me, so quickly.

Hell, I remember joking with my friend as I passed him in the hall freshman year. I remarked at the fuss over him, not understanding it. He was skinny, all spindly arms and a mouth too big for his face. His eyes were too small, and his voice cracked every time he spoke. He was a late bloomer; his beauty was ready to wound us though.

Sophomore year Bryan got his braces off. And he grew taller every damn summer.

My infatuation, my obsession, was instantaneous. I had come out of the restroom at a basketball game. He was arriving late, running down the hall.

Suddenly I was on the floor, and he was on top of me. Just for a second, I felt all of him. Warm skin and his voice near my ear. Unintentional, but devastating. He jumped to his feet, reached for my elbow, and hauled me upright.

"I'm so sorry, so so sorry," he muttered.

I never knew the color of his eyes before that moment. Navy blue, wide and worried about me. Heavy brows and full lips so close I could reach out and touch them. I was done for. A goner. Stick a fucking fork in me.

"It's okay," I managed. His hand was still on my elbow, those long slender fingers wrapped around it.

I looked down at them. Pale and soft. His eyes followed, and he dropped my elbow quickly, rushed past me.

I kept my eyes on him the rest of the night. Watched him run back and forth across the court. I didn't tell my friends, Akia, Britt, and Christina, of my crush until a few weeks later. My sudden interest in basketball games finally made sense to them. When I confessed, they laughed at me, knowing full well how useless it was to be in love with a boy like him, so above us.

Mrs. Michaels returned, pulling me from my memory. It felt like a bucket of cold water had been dropped on me. She smiled at me, and I mirrored her. She was my favorite teacher, and I sometimes worried she suspected my crush, had observed my lamely disguised wanting and watching. It was her job to pay attention to us.

The bell rang before she made it to her desk, and the students started to stir, picking up their tests, bringing them to my desk.

I reached for my backpack on the floor. I didn't need to stay for this. My desk was merely the landing place for finished and unfinished tests. I slipped between two students, making my escape. I didn't want to be there when Bryan walked up. I didn't need to be set on fire again.

————

It would be simple, right? Hijack homecoming. That's what we called it a week later when the plan arose. We didn't want to see the same faces competing for the crown. We didn't want to stand in the shadows anymore.

"Okay. We have four crowns to capture," Christina said. She held up her hand and listed them off as she leaned against the back wall. At the top of the bleachers, we could see the entire school, assembled, ready to vote for an arbitrary crown that always went to the same names. Maybe it would work. Maybe we could pull this off. I looked down at the popular girls below us, laughing and looking like porcelain dolls. Aurora, Amy, Jenny, Angela, and the new foreign exchange student they took in, Luta. My eyes pulled from their perfect hair and perfect skin, to the rest of our class.

I wrote in my notebook as my friend spoke. "Fall Fest Queen. Miss Merry Christmas. Homecoming Queen. Prom Queen."

I dotted my last period and looked up from my papers. "This isn't going to work." I sounded as defeated as I felt. I was fiery when it came to battles we could win. This was out of our league.

"Yes, it will," my other friend Britt said, with a light in her eyes. "We outnumber them. It's simple math. What have the popular kids done for anyone but themselves? They have all the trophies from every year. Every crown. I'm sick and tired of it. It's time we took control of this." Britt loved control. She was a science nerd, and I had the unfortunate luck of being her lab partner junior year. My artistic, flighty mind did not mix well with her type-A traits.

And maybe I agreed with her. Some part of me thought it would work, but I feared the crash. I feared for the first of us, putting ourselves out there only to fail. It would be humiliating. And the popular girls would never let us live it down if they caught on to what we were doing.

Then, I thought about the guys. Who would be nominated on their end? I looked over at my three friends and tried to guess who we would nominate for which crown, how we would choose.

Prom, for example, would be a bigger crown, both physically and metaphorically, than Fall Festival. Akia answered my question as she reached for my notebook.

"Okay, so let's write them on pieces of paper. Britt, give me your hat. We'll throw them in and pick. That way it's fair."

I handed my notebook over and sucked in a breath. I didn't want Akia to flip to the poem I wrote during study hall about Bryan.

They all knew about my all-consuming crush on our classmate, the most popular boy in school, and our star basketball player, but I didn't want them to see my lame rhymes and longing.

Across the gym, I caught Bryan's eyes. He was turned around, talking to dickhead jock Rodney Bartholomew, but he was watching me. I blushed and looked back at my friends.

Why did he always have to stare? I wanted him to stop, or act on it.

When Akia finished, she tossed the tiny folded scraps of paper that held our fate into Britt's hat. Christina went first, reaching in, grabbing hers. "Do I open it now?" she asked.

"No, wait. Let's all pick and open ours at once," Akia answered. We nodded, murmuring our consent.

When I reached in, I felt the hairs on my arms lift. Was Bryan looking again? I didn't investigate. I couldn't let him see me staring back for the twentieth damn time today. I had some pride. Some.

My thumb ran over the tiny scrap of paper, over and over, as I waited for my friends to pick their fates. We all leaned back in our seats, silent, lost in our own unique thoughts. Perhaps all mulling over our escort options if we were lucky enough to choose Homecoming Queen. Fall Fest and Miss Merry Christmas nominees didn't have school dances erected in their honor. And the prom candidate would walk in with one of our male classmates who was nominated.

We all had crushes, no boyfriends. Akia couldn't ask her crush to walk her in since she spent the better half of French lusting over Mr. Arseneau, with his full head of hair and lulling accent. Britt spent most hours in between classes giving us play by plays of her latest sighting of Ritchie Tenfield, a Burlingame High graduate who came home on the weekends to visit his family from the community college he attended in Topeka. And Christina, she was in purgatory, like me. Her crush, going six months strong now, was on Rodney. He was one of Bryan's best friends, our baseball team's pitcher, and a complete dick. In my opinion, and in Akia's opinion, and in Britt's opinion, most days. She often tried to play mediator or to pacify Christina when she was upset with us for pointing out his multitude of flaws. Love was blind, I knew that well enough. But was it deaf too? His loud booming voice grated on me.

Down on the gym floor, I saw our principal talking to Mrs. Michaels. "Guys, we better get this going. We better pick and start talking to everyone if we plan to pull this miracle off." I pulled my hand up and tapped my tiny paper to my forehead. For luck? I didn't know.

"Okay. Yes. Let's do this." Britt bounced in her seat. "One. Two. Three." I watched her open her paper. Then Christina. Then Akia. I watched their faces. The multitude of emotions rippling.

I pulled my eyes away, locked onto my long white fingers. I gripped the paper so tight it hurt. Slowly I let the pressure release, unfolding, opening my fate. I heard my friends murmuring, naming their crowns, their goals. It was all jumbled, garbled, white noise.

"Sev, we need to get down there and start talking to everyone! Britt needs to take Fall Fest Queen. We need to start on a good note. We need to take this first one. That confidence is going to help us take the others!" Akia was electric, excited. "Are you okay?"

I looked up, away from my paper. "No," I whispered. And then louder, "How the fuck am I going to get nominated for Homecoming Queen?"

And how am I going to get the guts to ask Bryan to escort me in, in front of the entire school?

NOT FRIENDS, NOT LOVERS

My old house looks the same. White shutters and yellow siding. When I walk in, I can hear the attic fan going. The whoosh of air I always associated with the blistering Kansas heat. So many open fields, no reprieve. Nothing to stop the memories from finding me.

My father never believed putting in air conditioning was a necessity. He could afford it if he saved. But there was always something else he placed first.

Our college savings.

New school clothes.

Sasha's first car.

I remember hot summer nights falling asleep in my underwear; a box fan shoved in the window. The one above my bed whirling as well, lulling me to sleep, singing with the cicadas.

How could I have forgotten this? All the clothes I packed to sleep in are taking up valuable space I could have used for something else. It's too hot for that shit.

I try to ignore the sound of construction across the street, but all the open windows make it difficult. They betray me. He never was easy to hide from. I had to move away to feel unwatched.

Maybe I'll escape to my car, turn the air on, the sound up.

Of all the people and things I thought I'd have to face when I came home, he was the one I dreaded most. Well, him or Aurora, or the one I cannot speak of.

I find my room, and it makes my heart thunder in my chest. I've stepped into a time capsule. Nothing has changed. My pale-yellow bedspread is sitting on my full-size bed, and ivory wrought iron scales the wall, still covered in striped wallpaper.

To the right is my nightstand, made of stacked suitcases I found at flea markets with my father on our weekend adventures. To the left is a peeling NSYNC poster. I should pull it off the wall, but I leave it and walk to my little vanity, next to my dresser. My jewelry box is sitting on top. When I open it, a tiny ballerina twirls.

My father kept me happy, whole, fed, and growing in this house. What will become of it now that he no longer lives here? I should have come home. More than never. At least a few times. It was self-ish, stupid. I didn't have the money to drop everything, and I convinced myself that was a good enough reason. A lie can be a good reason if you repeat it over and over again.

Sasha has been home. But she is motherly. She had to be. She raised me until she left home. That habit never left her. She is still that woman, always caring for me, no matter the miles.

My father is just a few blocks away, and I'm terrified to see him in a couple of hours. To see how far he has fallen. My aunt says he has more good days than bad. But the bad ones are often.

He remembers the war. The friends he lost.

He remembers losing my mother.

And on the tough days, he forgets losing her, and won't rest until someone tells him where she is.

There are even days when he forgets he has two daughters, and he thinks he has a son. This is how I learned my parents had a miscarriage before my sister and me. More than one.

It shouldn't be surprising. They had me so late in their lives.

I walk to my bed and fall back onto it—a trust fall into my past. A light puff of dust flies up, swirls around me, and is ripped away by the fan.

The sound of a hammer makes its way to my ears when everything settles, as I close my eyes. I wanted to take a small nap before getting around, but that's not going to happen. I have business to take care of.

I need to see Bryan.

———

Twenty minutes later I cross my lawn, cross my street, walk onto the school property. I don't know where my nerve comes from, but I want to see his face and his reaction. I want to store it away with every other memory of him.

They say everything looks smaller when you come home. It does. Smaller and sadder. There is a melancholy laced in the smallness of this place. Maybe it isn't there for everyone, but not everyone has lost all that I have. Not everyone left here, scarred and shaking.

I walk into the school and take in my surroundings. My eyes need time to adjust, so I breathe, in and out. I clutch my chest, then laugh at my dramatics.

Tools and tarps litter the hallways. I hear loud banging, clanking sounds in the distance. A hammer to a wall.

Somewhere near my old English class seems to be where the noise is originating. I wonder if it's Bryan. This project can't be a one-man job. What if someone else is in here and I get caught trespassing? I'll just blame it on nostalgia. On wanting to see my old desk, my old locker, my past captured in brick.

I'm playing with fire here; this is the truest thing I know. But I was always with him, the break in time and miles hasn't lessened this need. This need to play. A toxic trait I need to exhume.

My feet are covered in sawdust when I glance down. I reach for the wall and let it guide me, watching my step, less brave than I wish I could be.

I turn the corner to step into the classroom, and I pull my eyes up. I see Bryan's back, his hips, his calves—the shape of him I'll never be able to scrub from my brain.

He has headphones in, and he's sanding down drywall. His hammer is at his feet. I know I need to make some noise, to stop creeping around, so I reach for the light switch and flick it up and down, causing his body to whip around. When his eyes meet mine, they are not kind.

I break the silence, pulling my hand up in a small wave. "Hi."

He drops the sanding brick in his hand. "How did you get in?"

"The main door was unlocked. Was it not supposed to be?"

"Richard was supposed to lock it." Terse words. Dismissive and biting. Fitting for someone who fled, who never learned how to say goodbye. But sometimes an ending cannot be given. Sometimes the ones we place on pedestals lose our trust.

"Who's Richard?" I ignore his tone. Our missing goodbye plays in my head, all the scenarios I ran away from, avoided.

"My uncle. He bought the school." He crosses his arms.

"So he has money, eh?" Dumb question, filler mostly. I want to touch him, hug him. The need is surprising, annoying. I scratch my arm so I can feel something.

"You'd be surprised how cheap this place went for on the court-house steps. It was auctioned off. And in worse shape than you'd think."

"I'm sure it'll look great when you're done fixing everything up." I talk as though we're friends. As though we're catching up, and everything is erased. He won't allow it.

He clears his throat. "What are you doing here, Sev?"

No one has called me Sev in years. My body reacts to the moniker in a way I refuse to dissect. I reach up, pinch the bridge of my nose. "I wanted to come see how you've been. How you are."

He laughs, but there is no warmth there.

There are still school desks in the classroom. I see our old teacher's desk shoved against the blackboard. I walk to it, hoist myself up.

Bryan takes a seat at one of the small desks close to the window. He reaches out to a glass full of dark liquid on the windowsill.

"I shouldn't be talking to you." No mincing words. They echo sentences offered to me in the past, in our past. We are doomed to repeat our mistakes unless we face them. My father told me that, back when he was able to give advice. What will he be able to give me when I see him later today? I frown and bury my head in my hands. I can feel Bryan; he swells in the room.

I wish for nothing more than to touch him once again. Just once.

The brush of a hand.

The graze of an arm.

He is still beautiful and the realization that I still want him hits me all at once.

"Why shouldn't you be talking to me?" *Don't say it. Don't.* He does.

"Aurora."

The name chills me. The one girl who had everything I ever wanted.

"You guys are still together?" I knew they got married. Facebook is a glorious and horrible thing.

"Not quite." He leans back in the seat.

I feel transported. Fixated.

He was always that way—leaning back, making me stare. So comfortable in his skin, never in his work or his mind, but his flesh, he lived in it so entirely.

His eyes hold no mischief now. Not like they used to.

"What's '*not quite*' mean?" I edge.

He looks down at his shoes. "Separated. At the moment."

"I'm sorry." My mind races, the way it always does. Trying to find my in. My plan and all the ways I can approach this. I miss the old schemes, I miss my old friends. I have no one in my corner to help me figure this out.

"Are you?" He challenges me.

I am. I *am* sorry to hear it. I find no delight in knowing they're not doing well, if only for the sake of the child I know they had together. "Yes." I stare into his eyes, embrace the burn of them. He can give me his malice. I will eat it up. "Why wouldn't I be? You think I'm still harboring a high school crush?" I am. Will it ever die? Or will it always lie dormant, in wait for my weak moments?

"Well, it's not like you've thought of me since graduation. The whole world knows you haven't." He throws his arms out wide. He always had an impressive wingspan. I remember his arms around me, the temporary warmth of him.

I roll my eyes before I can stop myself. I should have known it would come up, the screenplay I penned in college. *Not Friends, Not Lovers*. "I wrote it. I didn't star in it. It was an indie film, not some blockbuster. So don't act like it was some scandalous thing. To everyone else, it was just some movie. Some made-up story."

"Did you hate me that much?"

"Hate you? What do you mean?" The light I cast on him was unflattering. I was wounded, recovering from everything. So I aimed my anger at him. I couldn't aim it at the one I would never name. The one I forced myself to never speak of.

"I was just some dumb jock. And Aurora, a mean girl."

I shrug my shoulder at his defense of her. He never saw her the way the rest of us did. "Well, maybe that's what she was back then. What, did you guys watch it together?"

"Fuck no. She watched it though. And obsessed over it. Obsessed over those years and what I did to her. It's why we are where we are." I hear it there as it rolls off his tongue—the blame. I'm to blame for all his woes. So like him to place blame anywhere he can stake it.

"And this is the reason for your bitchy attitude toward me?" I hop off the desk, pace in front of the blackboard. My index finger reaches for the dust and chalk. I draw a line.

"Yeah, I guess you could say that."

"Don't blame me for the fact that you cheated on your girlfriend when you were eighteen. I didn't do that." I draw a heart, scribble a jagged line down the middle.

"Maybe not. But you weren't innocent either. It wouldn't have happened without you there."

I whip around at his words, a flurry of dander and chalk floats in the air. "Are you fucking kidding me? I didn't make you cheat. I wasn't seducing you." My sharp mouth, my callous words, they fall out. My father always told me to watch my language on the phone. I never listened.

"You weren't?"

"No. Are you kidding me? Is that really how you want to paint it? Fuck off." I leave the classroom in a haze of anger and red. My sandals flip and flop on the tile, an embarrassing retreat.

I hear Bryan following me, the push of the desk across the room.

"Why did you have to write about it?" His words echo across the hallway.

I spin, face his approaching form. "Why wouldn't I? I left Kansas and moved to a city where I knew no one but my sister. I had nothing but this broken heart and a story to tell. That's what we do, that's what writers do. We tell our stories."

"Regardless of who gets hurt?"

"Yes. Regardless of who gets hurt. Life's a bitch, and I'm not going to sit on the past that I own to save *your* feelings, or hers. You didn't give two shits about her feelings so why should I have?" We don't speak of the elephant in the room. The real reason my heart broke and why I left with no goodbye. His loyalties lie with the wrong people.

"I did care about her feelings." It sounds hallow, and we both hear it. I see it in his eyes, the reflection.

"You had a funny way of showing it." I hear our moans, the sound of our clothes hitting the ground. So close. We were so close.

"I cared about you, too, once. I couldn't stay away, and I'm sorry. Am I ever going to stop paying for what I did when I was a dumbass kid? That was over ten years ago. When does it end?" His fingers are running through his short hair; he's talking to the wall now, avoiding my eyes.

"Don't know. Don't care. That's for you two to figure out. I'm not playing the middle woman anymore." Can I convince myself of another lie? What's one more, really?

"That's not why you came over here?"

"No. I wanted to say hi to an old friend." I would have taken his friendship, but I wasn't even worthy of that. Not by the rules of

Burlingame High. And here we stood, surrounded by these haunting halls.

"Friend? We've never been friends. You know that. We are not friends." It stings.

I walk backward, my hands up in defeat. When I've stepped over the threshold dividing Burlingame High and the front lawn, I laugh. "And not lovers. Was that your next line?"

"Yeah, maybe it was." He closes the door in my face.

SUCK IT UP

PAST

We piled into the gym, one by one, side by side, large groups. I shot off a manic prayer to the man upstairs after we voted for Homecoming candidates, a half hour ago, and my reward was a scheduled tornado drill. That distraction gave me more time to work myself up. I was being taught a lesson. Thanks, God.

Christina held my hand, trying to calm my nerves. I thought I might puke and turned an ugly shade of pea green. I was sweating in January. My birthday was nearly here, and I couldn't believe I was about to turn eighteen. I was an almost eighteen-year-old virgin with no car and an all-consuming crush that was about to fucking crush me.

There were a lot of things in life that didn't make sense to me. The way crickets scared the shit out of me. The way my father could eat twice as much food as me and never gain a pound. Compound fractions. The fact that none of my friends loved the Harry Potter books as much as I did.

I could now add the fact that my friends and I had pulled off the biggest social status underdog wins in Burlingame High School history.

First, Britt took Fall Fest. Then Akia took Miss Merry Christmas. Homecoming was fast approaching. It was time to pick a nominee, and I had miraculously pulled that slip out of the hat that fateful fall day with my best friends.

I felt sicker and sicker to my stomach with every week that went by. Every moment we got closer to the day voting started, to about twenty minutes ago.

The popular girls were on to our game, and they were not happy with us. A few weeks ago, Aurora Trent shoved me into a locker when she saw me laughing at one of Akia's jokes. When I turned back to her, she hissed at me, and that shut me right up.

Aurora was five-eleven to my five-one. I wasn't going to look at her funny or cross her. I knew better. In second grade, she stuck a piece of gum in my hair, and I had to cut my hair. Six inches, gone.

I still couldn't look her in the eye.

Knowing that she was showing interest in Bryan these days made things reach a new level of massively shitty.

Whatever Aurora wanted, Aurora got. I didn't stand a damn chance. We all knew it, we just rarely spoke of it. It was too depressing.

I had been watching them in the hallways for three weeks, and they were always close, the way they are now. I stumbled over my feet, watching them. Akia grabbed my arm and steadied me.

We found a spot at the top of the bleachers, our spot. Below, the class president, Erica, was down on the gym floor, staring up into the crowd. When she locked eyes with me her lips turned up at the corner, and I felt a wash of heat flow over my body, from my top to my toes. *Fuck. How was this going to go?*

Sometimes the one thing you want is actually what you don't want, when you think about it long enough. I didn't like to be the center of attention. I was a writer, and a performer only when it was absolutely necessary. And only on the theater stage. I wanted to be in the back. I wanted to be behind the curtain, giving cues, giving advice on how to speak lines, how to walk across the stage.

I didn't like to be out in the open. I didn't want the whole school to look at me as I walked across that gymnasium floor.

I turned to Christina and stared at her, wide-eyed and white as a sheet. I could feel the color draining from my skin.

"What?" She looked around, searching for what may have pushed me further into my hysteria.

"This isn't some sort of weird self-confidence thing, or ego playing out in real time. But, I think I'm going to win this. We have been making this happen, and I know this is a bigger crown, but I can feel it. I'm going to get nominated, and I don't know if I can do this. This isn't just a parade or anything. This is Homecoming. And it all sounded so cool in my head when I played it out. I would get nominated and then I would ask Bryan to be my escort, and he would fall head over heels in love with me, and we would spend the rest of high school attached at the face, and maybe groins—if I'm feeling ambitious, but now, this is *real!* I can't do this. Erica just practically winked at me from down there, and she has the results in her hand. What the fuck? Why did we do this?" I aimed for a whisper, but my pitch was all wrong. People around us started to turn their heads and Christina placed her palm on my lips to stop me.

"Whoa, whoa, whoa. You need to pull it together. It won't be the end of the world if this happens. And yes, I think it'll happen, too.

But we gotta keep it together. We have to act like this doesn't scare us at all. Because the Junior Class? They're looking at us. And the Sophomore Class? Same there. We made this happen, and this is showing everyone who will come after us that the old rules, they don't have to apply. We can change things when we band together. So suck it up and be brave. Be fucking brave. Okay?"

I shook my head up and down; the vibration of a microphone being turned on made me jump.

"Okay, ya'll! Burlingame High! Are we excited to find out which lucky ladies are going to be our Homecoming Queen candidates?" Erica's voice boomed around us and I shot forward in my seat. My sweaty palms grabbed onto the bleachers.

They would start at the Freshman Class and work their way up. Torture. Sweet, typical torture. That's all high school was really.

The voices melted together, and I retreated inside. My eyes aimlessly wandered, finally landing on the back of Bryan's head. I could see that he was hunched low in his seat, his knee bopped up and down. It was a nervous habit of his. I had seen him do it when working on essay questions in English class.

I looked down at my own knee, jumping up and down like a grasshopper. I stilled it with my hand like it was a foreign entity. I barely felt in control of my own body.

I had no release for this stress, and the climb was too much. I needed this over, so I could process whatever came from our plan.

I focused on the voices filling the gym. The Junior Class candidate was just announced, we were so close.

My stomach lurched, and I leaned forward, pushing my face into Britt's hair. She reached back, pinching my nose and making me chuckle.

Erica stepped forward, taking the microphone back from the Junior Class President as their class slowed their clapping. I pushed back in my seat and pulled the hood of my sweatshirt over my head.

"Okay, Senior Class. This is the moment we have all been waiting for. Are you ready to hear who will be representing the girls as homecoming candidate?"

Cheers and wolf whistles echoed around the gymnasium.

Erica waved the microphone in the air and hopped up and down, reveling in the energy swirling around us.

"Okay. Without further ado, I present to you, the Senior Class candidate...our very own Miss Severin Thompson!"

The ringing was immediate. My ears burned hot and every sound melted together. I felt hands on my arms, my shoulders, and I rocked back and forth in my seat, a hysterical laugh pulled from my throat. When I pulled my hood back and looked into the crowd my eyes landed on Bryan again.

And he was smiling.

WHERE IS YOUR ROOM?

MY FATHER'S HANDS ARE WORN. THERE IS NOTHING delicate about them. They are strong, they always have been. They are working hands, hands that have held me when I fell. Hands that fixed scratched knees, broken refrigerator doors. Hands that brought in the groceries.

His hands are worn and they feel weak. It is cruel, the way this disease steals from us.

I look into my father's eyes and search for recognition.

Something. Anything. He smiles and I will not cry. This cannot happen.

"I love you. A million miles and back." It was always our thing to say. My sister repeats the saying, seated next to me, gripping my hand. She has been back in Burlingame with me for two weeks.

My father's eyes stay on mine. A smile plays on the corner of his mouth, then his eyes drift over my shoulder.

He was mine for a second. Now he's gone. Lost in the conversations going on around us.

I hear the home director tell the other residents they can join her outside for lunch. It's cooler today, in the sixties. It'll be good for them.

I stand, never letting go of my father's hand. Sasha goes to his other side, laces her arm into his.

When we make it outside he drops my hand, walks over to Clarice, another resident.

Anne, the home director, makes her way to us. "He will have good days, and he will have bad days. He will have days in between. You never know what you will find."

"Is he happy here? Truly? It's hard for me to tell. This isn't any normal I thought I would ever have to accept. I know him at home. Being in charge. Being in control." My sister's voice is aching.

"I believe so," Anne assures. "It's not the life he had, but he can never go back to that. And it would only frustrate and confuse him."

"So, it's kind of like a clean slate here?" I feel no relief, but I try to mask that. No happiness finds me when I cling to the past, so I'm trying to let go. One visit at a time.

My father loved to take care of himself, his sister, my sister, and me. Until we left. Left him to fall victim to this disease.

We tell Anne goodbye, hug my father, and walk out of the courtyard. Home is a few blocks away. I grab my sister's hand as soon as we hit the sidewalk. We say nothing the whole walk, listening to our feet on the ground. I know she will get back to the house and call her girlfriend. She has a family back in New York to turn to. I wish I had someone to confide in like that.

Before I get to my house I let go, I tell Sasha with my eyes, where I'm going. She nods and lets me, bringing Beau in from the front porch for me.

Bryan's truck is parked on the lawn still, beckoning me. I'm tired of his cold stare, his fire tongue. Two weeks of this game has been enough.

I walk into the school, my ears opening, searching for the sound of a hammer, a saw, anything. I hear banging above my head.

My legs burn as I take the stairs, two steps at a time. I find him in the old auditorium. My home. My place in this school. The only room I felt like I belonged in.

I enter through the back, my fingers trailing the worn audience seats.

He is on the stage, bent low, a hammer in his hand.

I watch the muscles in his back work, he is unaware of me, and it takes me back. All of my unknown watching.

I find the door to the left of the stage, turn the knob carefully. It probably isn't smart to sneak up on someone while they are using a hammer, but I can't stop myself.

He pivots, glancing over his shoulder when I step onto the stage. It always creaked.

I still, drop my hands. They had been clasped, pulled close to my mouth.

"What do you want?" He sounds tired. Tired of me and my presence.

"To fight with you." It's an honest answer. I like watching his face take it in.

"You want that?"

"No. I don't like fighting with you. But I need it right now. I need to be mad at someone. I need a place for my anger to go."

"Let's have it then." He drops the hammer to the floor. The clatter echoes around us.

When he stands, he turns to me. I eye his sweat, his twitching jaw.

I want to touch him. I always want to touch him.

"Why do you hate me?" I know he doesn't, but it seems that way. The reasons for the hate I assume he holds, they don't compare to what I have in my chest. To my resentment.

"I don't. I just wish you would go away. This town isn't yours anymore."

"Was it ever?" I laugh, and it is not kind. "It's always been your town and Aurora's town and your friends helped you rule it. Try again." And the one I won't speak of. He helped them rule. I blow out an angry breath, circle him.

"God." He sounds defeated. "Just leave me alone."

"I can't. Do you know why I'm here? Good fucking God, dude!" I know he knows. This town has ears, and though I've been hiding out since my return, they know I'm back. The town always knows.

"I know. I do. But you wanted to fight so I'm going to tell you every ugly thought you need to get this going, okay?"

"Just the sight of your face gets me going." So many meanings, I'm unwilling to let my face show him the truth of it.

"Oh, I have no doubt I get you going." He catches me and he is all smirk, white teeth. He needs to stop.

"Quit changing tactics." I roll my eyes. They damn near fall out of the back of my head.

"No, maybe this one will work better." He steps toward me, and I back away.

"Maybe what will work better?" I'm a live wire, frayed at the edges, bit off.

"A reminder. A reminder that you can puff your chest out all you want, throw me your anger, all that shit. But we both know it's because you can't stop wanting me. I could throw you down on this theater floor and fuck you if I wanted to. I could spread your legs, take it all."

I'm embarrassingly wet, already. "Your arrogance knows no bounds." My jaw is hard, tense.

He scoffs. "Please, we both know it's true. And we both know I'm not going to do a damn thing. I'm not going to touch you, Severin. I got everything I wanted from you back then. A kiss. A kiss was enough."

A montage of every touch, every bit of skin we bared flitters in my mind. "You did more than kiss me." He can't lie to me. We both know the truth. No one else does.

"Yeah, sure, some. But it all boils down to a kiss." He dismisses it, and the images swirl away. Angry orange and stifling, like this room.

"A kiss. Yeah, a kiss you started, buddy." I can still feel it. My bottom lip is burning.

"One you wanted, though." He is too close to me.

"And you." My words come out soft, mirroring my resistance. "You wanted it, too. That's the part you're leaving out."

"Everyone knows it. The town knows it. You know it. My wife knows it."

"If everyone knows it, why are you still beating yourself up for it?" It's in his tone. Self-loathing, leaking out all over the floor between us.

"I'm going to beat myself up for it until the damage is gone. Until everyone stops reminding me. Until you stop reminding me. And you're going to remind me of it, every time that movie plays. Every time you show up."

"Don't act surprised. You knew I was going to show up again. You're like a fucking magnet, dude."

"Are you going to keep doing that?"

"What?" It was an old trick. A fallback.

"Calling me dude, buddy. It's shit women do to remind a guy they don't want him. But it's just a little mask you're using, and we both can see right through it. So stop. How long were you in love with me?"

"In love?" I blanch. "Don't flatter yourself."

"You know what I mean." His shoulders go up and down, like he meant no offense, but holds no regret. His mouth is still mean, mischievous.

"I don't know. I think maybe freshman year is when I started to notice you." I'm softening. This isn't the fight I wanted. It has dissipated, fading like the red in my veins.

"Yeah, well, for me, it was kindergarten. That's when I noticed Aurora. Fucking five years old. And I even knew her before then. Maybe it was the comparison, and I was a little boy with a million crushes. But she was the cutest. The prettiest. She was already my best friend. Our grandmothers were best friends, and then they had daughters. They became best friends. It's almost like we were designed to be together."

Is he still trying to give me what I asked for? Barbs and a cutting edge? Or is this opening up? "So it was fate?" I never knew this, and I wish he wasn't telling me this story. The bite in my voice, the tremor, returns.

"I don't know. I know I liked you back then. So much. And then finally, finally she wanted me. Everything I wanted since I was a damn five-year-old was there, ready for me. You didn't stand a chance."

"You're not telling me anything I don't know. I knew I never stood a chance with you. And I think you're giving yourself too much credit."

"What do you mean?"

"Even if Aurora didn't want you. Even if everything lined up and we could have been together, we wouldn't have. You wouldn't have chosen me or dated me. You wouldn't have taken me to prom. I wasn't popular. I wasn't as pretty as the other girls, and I didn't wear the coolest clothes, I didn't play sports. This isn't some teen rom-com. I wasn't going to get some makeover, and you weren't going to tell your friends to fuck off. You were going to go along with what everyone wanted you to do. Because that's what you do. You listen to others, and you let them lead."

"Thank you." He walks away, to the edge of the stage.

"For what?" I follow him.

"For confirming every fear I've ever had about myself. For showing me you can see it. The weakness."

"I'm sorry. I was just, I was trying to show you I knew. That it never was going to be a thing with us." He takes a seat on the edge of the stage, in front of me, so I lower myself down next to him.

"Maybe in some alternate universe." He stares down at his worn jeans, his worn shoes.

"Thanks for that." I blow out a puff of air, half agreeing, half resentful.

"You know what I mean."

"Yeah, of course. I'm only desirable in a world where Aurora doesn't exist." Now he is confirming my fears.

"No, that's not what I mean."

"Quit backtracking now. It's the spine thing. Like I said back then," I bite, "you don't have one. You're caving now."

"You said that back then?" He laughs angrily. "No. No way. You weren't like this back then, you know?"

"Yeah. I know. It's called growing up. Confidence. It's called realizing that there is a big world out there and you can be whoever the fuck you want to be. High school doesn't mean anything. It's just a blip on the map of your life." I was more me, more in my skin than I had ever been. I liked this me. Would he?

"I feel like I never left. I'm friends with the same people, and I've been with the same girl, and I see the same teachers. Hell, I'm in the same damn school. Every day."

"How creepy is it? You live here, right?" I couldn't tell, with his truck always on the lawn, never moving. But at night, I saw lights on until late.

"Yes I live here. And you have no idea. So many sounds at night."

"Where is your room?" I regret the words as soon as they leave my mouth. They sound like a come-on.

If he notices, he doesn't show it. "The principal's office. It was the first room we finished. The closet is his old safe. So if there's ever a tornado in Burlingame, that's where I'm hiding."

The principal's office is at the front of the building. You can see the window from my front porch. I know I'll be watching now.

We sit like that for a while. The sound of our breaths, in and out, signals the passage of time. It's so awkward, and I have no idea what to do. I'm about to speak when the auditorium lights directly over the audience seats light up. They flicker and sputter, groaning. I pull my arm up and shield my eyes, registering Bryan rising to his feet, a flurry of curse words rising with him.

"What the hell are you doing in town?" a voice says.

I pull my arm down and see a guy about our age walking down the aisle, a shit-eating grin plastered on his face. I like his Vans, his nylon shorts. He's tall, and his hair is a little shaggy. A pair of aviators pushes it back, off his forehead. He looks familiar, and when he speaks, I recognize the voice. One of the last I heard before I left town. *Oh no.*

"Hey, brother. Sev, let me walk you out?"

My mind rushes to catch up as Ben Winthrop winks at me, before turning his gaze back to his brother's. "Aurora is on her way."

MINT & SWEAT

PAST

I LET TWO WEEKS PASS BEFORE I WORK UP THE NERVE TO talk to Bryan. They had to have been the worst two weeks of my life. And though I was often dramatic, I wasn't far off. Patience wasn't one of my strong suits, and I came home from school every day extra crabby. My father noticed and hovered until I told him it was just school stress. I wasn't lying. I was stressed about something, or someone, at school.

I waited by Bryan's truck for him to get out of basketball practice to pop the question he would surely laugh at, internally of course, because he wasn't a dick like his friends. I didn't know where else to ask him to be my escort. I still couldn't believe he failed to get nominated for Homecoming king. If we won the homecoming basketball game, it would most likely be because of him. He deserved a crown. He deserved to be in the spotlight. I didn't deserve this. I was feeling more and more like an imposter. Aurora and all her cronies were shooting daggers out of their eyes in my direction every day in gym class. I wanted to abdicate, and I didn't even have a crown or a damn throne.

When Bryan rounded the corner of his truck and found me leaning against his driver's side door, I yelped. I was so lost in thought. I never heard him coming.

"Oh, hey." He didn't smile. He stood still, looking me up and down. I saw heat in his dark blue eyes. I had never been this close to him.

I crossed my arm over my chest, feigning confidence, and pushed off his vehicle.

"Hi." An awkward moment went by where we just looked into each other's eyes. I was an idiot every time I was in his orbit. *Speak. Say something!*

I needed to move. I was in his way, and he was going to stay frozen in his tracks if I didn't woman up and talk, so I stepped away, the gravel crunching under my sneakers. "Sorry to startle you. I need to ask you a question." At least I didn't say *can I ask you a question?* I hated when people did that.

He went for his door, opened it, and threw his gym bag into the back seat.

This was a dumb idea. This was the dumbest fucking idea I ever drummed up in my life.

I pushed a spider web off his truck, the silver shining under the streetlight, just under the mirror. I was looking for anything to keep me distracted. When I looked up, Bryan was leaning against his door, in the same spot I had just left. Could he feel the heat of my body there still?

"What's that?" He bit his lip, and I was back in his English class again. Watching him torture me. Squirming, with sweaty palms and other embarrassing bodily functions overcoming my self-control. I shifted my weight and cleared my throat.

"So, as you know," I was suddenly talking with my hands, something I only did in front of my friends, "I was nominated for the Homecoming Queen Senior Class representative. And I guess I need an escort. Someone to walk me into the middle of the gym for the crowning and all that. So, I was hoping you wouldn't mind doing that for me? Since you didn't get nominated." What. The. Fuck. Was. Wrong. With. Me? Why did I have to say it like that? Like I was holding something over him?

I wanted to run away. Just run the hell home right that instant. He could tell all his friends that I was a freak and I wouldn't win, which, who was I kidding, I wasn't winning this shit.

I huffed out a breath and stared up into the sky. How red were my freckled cheeks? I hated myself. I wanted to pretend this was all a dream. I pinched myself on the arm discreetly. Nope. I was awake. No getting out of this one.

"I'd love to."

I blinked in response and looked down, away from the sky. My hand went to my throat. "Okay. Thank you." I turned on my heel, started walking into the night. I needed to get out of there before he realized he said yes. Right on cue, he called after me.

"Sev?" He didn't use my full name. He called me by what my friends called me.

"Yes?" I turned back, eyes wide and sweat on my brow.

"So, I can't dress up. Because I'll be playing the game. I hope that's okay." There was a tone you used with people you knew. So different from the one used with people you saw day to day that did not know you intimately. His tone was somewhere in the middle. I felt a chill.

"That's okay." I shook my head back and forth.

"What are you wearing?"

"I don't know. I haven't bought a dress yet." Just a few sentences, but I was flying high. We were talking. Really talking. We never talked. We looked at each other from across rooms. We brushed each other in the halls, sometimes. I found myself walking closer, pulled in.

"I'm sure it'll look great." He couldn't know what his words would do. The way I would latch onto that. I would write poetry about it. Analyze it with Akia, and Britt, and Christina. I blushed, then looked away. I was smiling. All teeth and my biggest temptation right there. So close.

"Thanks." We both turned as more basketball players walked out of the west entrance. Bryan's posture stiffened, and I felt my stomach drop. "Okay. Well, I better get home." I hitched my thumb over my shoulder, pointing in the direction of my little yellow house. So different from the one he lived in.

"You're walking, right? Just across the street?"

"Yeah. I live in that house."

"You don't need a ride?"

"No. It's just right there." I pointed into the dark. When I turned back, I saw Bryan's younger brother, Ben, walking toward us. A strange smirk on his face. I could see his braces.

"Yeah, but it's dark," Bryan said, pulling my eyes back to him. "And people die on the road every day." I thought of being in his truck. Stuck in a small space with nothing but the scent of his mint breath, his sweat. And now I knew Ben would be in there, too.

"No, that's okay. Thank you though." I waved, then walked away, shivering in the night. I could feel their eyes on me until I stepped onto my porch steps. I didn't hear his truck start, the old engine unmistakable, until I closed the door.

HOLLYWOOD

EVERYTHING IN BURLINGAME IS WITHIN WALKING distance.

I step off the school porch and take a right, walking the two blocks that lead me to the main street. I hear Ben following, just a few steps back.

I see Faye's Diner, Abel's General Store, and Allen's Grocery.

It's a time warp. Everything is so close, and the price tags don't cause you to double over in shock, not compared to LA prices.

Ben pulls ahead of me and walks to Thompson Books, stopping at a cart of paperbacks on the sidewalk. His gravity is strong, like his brother's. They look so alike now. He's grown up, nearly as handsome as Bryan now. Broad shouldered, with a wide smile and full lips.

"What are you up to today? Other than splitting up conversations." I call after him. I can't spend time with him. He's not why I'm here, but I'm curious about him. He doesn't seem intent on wounding me with resentment over absent goodbyes.

"A little light reading. Maybe you can help me figure out the big words, Miss Writer." He waves the book in his hand in front of my face.

I snatch it, my fingers grazing his.

Zen and the Art of Motorcycle Maintenance. The pages blow air in my face as my thumb buzzes through them. It feels good. The day is already stifling.

"Can't. I'm busy." I'm not. There's nothing to do here, and I'm not sure I can handle another visit with my father for a day or two. I feel worn and raw.

"Yeah, me, too." He pulls a piece of paper from his back pocket. I snatch it.

"Who makes paper lists these days?" I scan the pages, finding nothing interesting.

"People who aren't living on their cell phones. You should try it sometime."

Am I obsessed with my cell phone? Sure. But no more than anyone else these days. Being back in Burlingame makes it feel like a strange object from a distant future. Plus, the service is shitty here. When I'm back in my old room, I have to make sure I prop it near the window, and it's at the perfect angle, to ensure I get texts and alerts.

I push Ben's list back into his chest. He grabs it, and his fingers graze mine this time. I see Mrs. Forrester, the town lawyer's secretary, eye us through the glass, her eyebrow raising.

I'm going to be hot gossip in no time. How did this happen? How did I get out here in the open? I was doing so good at staying put, hidden away. One look at Ben and I'm walking the cobblestone streets, showing everyone I'm back. That it wasn't a rumor. I'll be the talk of the town when I leave.

And I will leave. I need to remind myself of this.

My life is not here and it never will be again.

I brush past Ben, pulling my cell phone from the small cross-body purse hanging by my hip. I hear his footsteps behind me.

"Where to first, Sevvy?" The name makes my steps slow for a minute. I think of prom, yellow tulle, ringlets in my hair, baby's breath. I shrug my shoulders, and the memories slip away. "I'm getting some groceries."

"Do you have any idea how overpriced they are there?"

"Yes, compared to local big cities," I use air quotes like the jackass I am, "but I don't feel like driving to Topeka. And my aunt says the Auburn Apple Market grocery is closed down."

"So you're just going to overpay? Ah, well, we all know you have the money."

I hear the implication. Small towns and small minds romanticized Hollywood and Orange County. "Just because I live in LA doesn't mean I'm loaded."

"But they made that thing you wrote into a movie." His voice is too similar to Bryan's. I don't like it.

"Also doesn't mean I'm loaded," I say, pushing the comparison away. I'm doing okay when it comes to money. I can pay my bills, and I put ten percent of everything I make into my savings account, just like my father taught me. I have no debt. I'm doing better than I was as a child. I wanted for nothing then, though, thanks to my father.

I think of his face. So long and with eyes that have dulled.

He is more than the disease, but he is losing. I'm going to lose him.

I suddenly have no patience for Ben and his following figure.

"Are you going to follow me around all day? Is that what's about to happen? Because I don't think I can take it today." I stop and square my stance, look up into his face. His eyes are wide, and his palms go up in surrender.

"Sorry. I had to get out of the house. I didn't expect to see you. And when I did, I thought, okay. This day won't suck."

"They all suck here." And not just because it was boring, but because it was quickly becoming a black hole.

"I'm not going to argue that. But I have my reasons. I'd wager a guess they differ from yours. Is it my brother? I can't believe that's back on." Wide grin again. I want to slap him.

But Bryan and I, who knows what is going on there? I let Ben believe that's the reason for my long face. I don't want to discuss my father right now. I nod.

"Hey, Hollywood. Don't take my shit so seriously." Ben is smirking, and I don't know how I feel about it. The warmth in my belly. It's familiar, being near him. And I wonder if it's due to the time I have spent with Bryan. They are a year apart, and their voices have a natural softness, one I crave when the world gets loud. I need caffeine. I need a reason for this buzzing. Something I can blame.

I look at his broad shoulders and dark denim. He is disheveled, unkempt in a way the kind of boys I'm drawn to never are.

When did I last see Ben Winthrop? I don't want to think about that week. I don't want to think of nameless people.

"Please don't call me that," I say. A little defeated.

"Why not? That's where you're from, right? Own it."

"Yeah, but I'm not like, Hollywood. Not the way you're saying it."

"Are you vegan? Do you do yoga?"

"Ben, people do that everywhere. That's not just an LA thing. Be more original." I walk away, no idea where I'm going.

"Hey, Sevvy, wait." I hear his Vans scratch across the sidewalk as he hurries to catch up.

I smile before I can stop myself, stop in my tracks. With a name like Severin, you're bound to be handed a few nicknames. It doesn't roll off the tongue easily. I turn to him and he pulls his palms up again, sweet surrender.

"What, Winny?" I laugh, giving my peace offering easily. He smiles and I want to hug him. To thank him for prom all over again.

"When did you get into town?" He starts walking down the sidewalk, so I follow.

"Two weeks ago, maybe a little more." Too much has happened already. I feel stretched thin and anxious. I need a drink or something. Anything to get a release. "I didn't know you still lived here."

"I don't. I'm home for the summer. College break."

I look up at him. "Still in college?"

"Yeah, that's what happens when you say you're not going and then change your mind and start late. Not all of us have things figured out when we leave this place, Sevvy."

I stop walking and take in the town square. My breathing is even, but my heart stutters. There appears to be a farmers' market near the gazebo and some sort of festival. I didn't expect to see a crowd.

I don't want to face this town, the people, just yet. I feel like something is waiting for me. A humiliation. An ambush.

I'm always waiting for someone to drop a vat of pig's blood on me or some shit like that.

"You okay?" Ben crosses his arms and arches a brow at me. His face is scruffy, more than a five o'clock shadow covers his skin. His forearms are tan.

"Yeah. I think. It's just, this town. I haven't seen anyone since I got back. Just my dad and my aunt. And your brother. What the hell is going on over there?" I wave my arms at the crowd.

"It's Summer Fest. Remember it? And how much have you seen my brother?" His tone is changed, his vibe, all of it shifts.

"Wait, what does that tone imply? I didn't even mean to see him. It wasn't some goal or anything. I live across from the school. Did you forget that?" I don't know why I'm explaining myself. It's an old habit. Explaining my time with Bryan, making excuses.

"We weren't friends in school. So, yeah. I guess I did." He is lying about forgetting. We both know it. He pauses, looking into the crowd of people with me. "So, what was that like?"

"What was what like?"

"Seeing my brother for the first time in years?"

"Weird. Like being in a room with a live wire. He has this animosity toward me. It wasn't fun." I have no words to describe it. But, I'm keyed up. It feels like there is a bat in my stomach, flying about. The butterfly feeling escaped us years ago.

"Over the movie?"

"Yeah. You know about the movie?"

Ben laughs, and it's hard to look away from. "Everyone does. My mom called me about it. She likes to tell me about everything that goes on here and everything that happens with Bryan. Like I care." He shrugs. "It's why I barely tell her anything about my private life or dating. Because I know she would be on the phone with Bryan an hour later telling him everything. Like either one of us cares about what the other is doing."

"Do you guys hate each other or something?" They were never the kind of brothers you saw talking in school or hanging out. With just a year separating them, I didn't see why. My sister was like my best friend, and we had many years between us.

"Yeah, ever since we were kids." I stare at him. He doesn't blink. "Okay, maybe hate is a strong word. I find him to be...annoying."

"I'm glad my sister doesn't feel that way about me."

"I'm sure your sister isn't a dick." He claps a hand on my shoulder. "Okay, Hollywood. You need to face this. You need to get out there and smile and say hi to people and remember that most old people won't even recognize you and this town is like half retirement home and half farmers' market." He points at the vegetable and pie stands.

I laugh, shrugging his hand off. "Okay. This is fine. It's fine." I'm lying to myself, and the thought that Aurora could be in the crowd makes my stomach lurch.

"The best part is you're walking in with me so everyone will be like, *'OMG she is with the other brother now! How will she mess up his life?!'*"

I turn to him so quickly he flinches.

His hands go up in surrender for a fight I haven't even started. "I was just joking!"

"Don't be an ass. What the fuck? I hadn't even thought of anything like that. So let's add that to the list, huh?" A few heads at the edge of the crowd turn toward my shrill tone. I wave meekly.

"Calm down."

"In the history of the words *calm* and *down*, how many times do you ever think that has worked to calm down a woman?"

"Maybe five or six times?" His teeth bite down on his lip, stifling a laugh that would have caused me to punch him.

I walk across the street, checking for traffic only when I'm halfway in the road. I hear Ben following, he calls to me, using my last name this time. "Thompson. Wait."

"How many different names are you going to call me today?" I call over my shoulder. "Pick one and stick with it."

"I reject constant and all it stands for."

I laugh at his word choice and freeze on the sidewalk. "Do you have any friends who are still here?" I only have one that stayed in Burlingame. I haven't spoken to Britt in years.

"You've lost your accent, you know?" He ignores my question. I jump right back at him.

"You have, too. Where are you going to college?"

"Connecticut. They say I have an accent there. Anywhere I go on the coasts, they say that. I don't hear it, but they do."

"It was always the same for me." My friends pointed out my accent, my word choice.

"You're stalling, Thompson."

"Hold my hand?" I fake a pleading tone. Well, it's half fake.

He reaches for me, and I pull my hand away. *I remember the last time he touched me.* "I was joking. I mean, like, metaphorically hold it."

"Walk with you?"

"Can you do that?"

Ben smiles wide, and I remember his braces in high school. *He's so grown up now, damn.* "Walk with my high school crush around town? I think I can handle that."

"Crush? Me? No." We start walking. I keep my eyes straight ahead, afraid they will meet with someone I don't want to see.

"Oh, please. You knew that. I spent half of prom making moon eyes at you."

"I didn't notice." A lie. I taste the liquor. Remember the night.

"I know. You were too busy staring at Bryan and Aurora and feeling sorry for yourself."

"Well. I couldn't help it. I don't hide things well. My feelings," I wave my hand in front of my face, "they just live there, for everyone to see, whether I want them to or not."

"I like that about you. Even when you don't want to say how you feel, it's all there."

"You think an awful lot about my face, don't you?"

"Don't flatter yourself. It's this town. Being here brings it all back. Memories and shit. I can recall prom like it was yesterday now. It's not the same for you?"

"Yeah, it is. I know what you mean. I've used the words time warp in my inner monologue a million times already."

"Inner monologue? Quit it." He play-punches me on the shoulder, and I try to swat his hand away, but I'm too slow.

"This is how I talk. Did that not come back to you, too?"

"It's all rushing back now." He nudges my shoulder, and I stumble a bit. He's always finding little ways to touch me, and I have no clue how I feel about it. Ben isn't his brother. He doesn't make my heart flutter, and I'm not sweating in his presence. Not the way I do when someone I find attractive is near. Well, I'm sweating but for an entirely different reason. The Kansas heat is going to be the death of me.

"You think Aurora is going to show up here when she's done with Bryan?"

"Are you curious about when you'll have to face her or are you curious about how long she is going to be alone with Bryan?"

I look up into his eyes. "Both."

We stand there for a moment, dissecting what it means. When I look into the crowd again, I see Aurora. Her arm is slung over the shoulder of a friend. It's not one of the usual suspects. It's my friend. It's Britt.

WHO'S YOUR DADDY

PAST

MOST SENIORS HAD FREE PERIODS. SOME STACKED THEIR classes, so they only had to go to school for half a day. I didn't have a car, so I chose to have my period right after lunch. I couldn't go home early. Yes, my house was within walking distance, but I didn't want to make that walk, rain, snow, or blistering sun. Also, my dad wasn't a fan of me lounging around the house half the day, if I was being honest.

It was lame, but I always ran to the auditorium for my free period. I practiced lines or tweaked my screenplays. I hid behind the curtain and wrote poetry. The time was never wasted. Not for me.

Today was not a good day for concentration, for quiet solitude. Technically, I was never alone. Desi Armand and Chet Holman always joined me on their free periods. Desi worked on homework in the seats, and Chet worked on his set. Arranging fake trees, organizing our costume department. Occasionally, other students would sit in the seating area, scattered randomly. But everyone kept to themselves, mostly.

I sat behind the giant red curtain that covered the stage. It was pulled back, and I hid on the right side, behind the gathered fabric.

Bryan was in the room. With Rodney, Mike, Brian with an I, and Nathan. A cluster of popular boys, chattering and laughing and not belonging here. I felt nervous, my foot tapped the stage floor as I wrote. My cursive was shit, and my hand ached. I had no idea what I was writing, but I was shit at distracting myself. I was listening to them speak, listening to their gossip. Did they know I was back here? I was always here. I lived for this room.

I didn't hear Bryan's voice. He was never the loud one, the flamboyant one. That was always Rodney. Rodney with his big calves, and his enormous arms and hands, and his spiky hair. He had fat lips and acne scarring on his neck. He was tall, six-three, and he drove the most beautiful car in the student parking lot. His father was a suit, he worked in Topeka, and his children and wife wanted for nothing. Rodney's mother was a stay-at-home mom, even though none of her kids were home to take care of.

I pulled my tapping foot from the stage, slipped it under my ass, and laid back. My skull made a gentle thump as it hit the old wood. My hands clutched my notebook to my chest. Bryan was my escort for the homecoming dance, yet I couldn't go out there and speak to him. When I got him alone, it was bearable. It was doable. But with his entourage, I was stuck. I was beneath him. In their eyes, anyway.

My name pulled me from my self-loathing.

"Just do it, man. It'll be hilarious." Rodney's voice boomed around the auditorium. Laughter echoed behind it, the sound of every voice. I didn't know if Bryan was laughing or not. He had a quiet laugh. You could see it in his eyes, in the way his shoulders shook. He wasn't loud in anything he did. In the way he moved or the way he spoke. He was quiet and beautiful.

Finally, I heard his voice. "Nah, man."

"C'mon. Don't be a pussy. Just, if she wins, which, let's be real, if she wins, what a fucking joke." More laughter followed, and I shot up, pushing my ear to the curtain. "If she wins, slap her on the ass and say 'who's your daddy!'"

"That doesn't even make sense." Bryan's tone was even, with a slight air of condescension. Or maybe that was just my imagination, my hope.

"It doesn't have to make sense. The point is to embarrass her. This shit has gone on long enough. And you know she is in love with you. So don't even deny that. We all do. She stares at you all the time. It's embarrassing."

"Embarrassing that a chick likes me?" I could hear the eye roll in Bryan's voice. I smiled.

"No. You know that's not what I mean, dumbass. It's embarrassing that she even thinks for a second that she has a chance with you." I didn't have to see his face to know what it looked like. Ugly and showing all the ugly in him.

"Harsh." Bryan sounded bored. I moved slowly, sliding my ass along the stage to the back. Where I knew I could push the curtain to the side, just slightly, for a visual.

"But then, you encouraged it, too. Saying you would be her escort."

"Let it go." I caught sight of them then. The other guys were watching the exchange. I'd always wondered about the power dynamics of the popular crowd. Aurora ruled the girls, but with the boys, it was unclear. Rodney was an alpha, through and through. It was in his walk, his talk, his stance. But he would never be as beautiful as Bryan. Every girl in school wanted to be by Bryan's side, in his bed, on their knees for him. And now, Aurora was sniffing around him in public. Everyone knew their families were close. That they spent some holidays together, and summer vacations. But at school, Aurora always seemed to have more power than him. He was not immune to her indifference.

"Whatever, man. If you don't want to put her in her place, I will." Rodney stood, his long legs stepped over the seat in front of him. Bryan crossed his arms, staring at his friend's retreated form.

"What are you going to do?"

Rodney turned, flashing his smile. It was the one thing he had going for him. It distracted from his ugly heart. I could see it, though others were blind to it. "I'll be up there, too. Don't forget that."

Maybe the answer was there. Who had the most power. Rodney was our Senior Class homecoming candidate. He wasn't the starting basketball player. He never racked up more points than Bryan, but he was our pitcher for the baseball team. And he was damn good. Bryan didn't play baseball. When he was in eighth grade, his father made him choose. Saying he could be okay in both sports, or excel in one.

I looked at Bryan's long legs, spread out in the seat. His broad shoulders and his square jaw. His face was a little red. "Don't." One word and it chilled me. I shivered from my spot on the stage.

"Why?" Rodney spun around, his arms wide. "She's just a theater geek. Don't piss away a good thing."

"What good thing is that?"

"Aurora. Don't tell me you haven't noticed her actually treating you like she gives two shits now."

"She's always treated me that way."

"Yeah, yeah, you're family, blah, blah. But now she's treating you like she gives a shit in *public*. We all know that's never happened."

"It's true, man." Nathan clapped his hand on Bryan's shoulder and he pulled his eyes from Rodney long enough to roll them at his other friend for encouraging Rodney.

"Do you like her?" Brian with an I spoke and Bryan turned to his other side. He was surrounded.

"Who?" Bryan's tone was annoyed. He shrugged the hands from his shoulder and stood, climbing over the seat in front of him to stand next to Rodney.

Rodney's booming laugh sent goosebumps up my arms. "The fact that you had to ask who is pretty scary, dude. Why would he be asking if you like Severin? First of all, you can't like a chick with a name like that." I scrunched up my face. Fuck you, Rodney. I liked my name. My mother gave it to me.

Bryan walked to the stage, leaned against it. His head fell to his chest, and he reached up to pinch the bridge of his nose. I wanted to walk out there. To halt it all. To be brave and unflinching. But that was something I would never be. I looked at Bryan, in all his beauty and turmoil. "I hate all of you. Seriously. She just asked me to be her escort and I said yes. It's not this big deal that you guys are making it out to be. Let it go."

"Just answer the question, then. And it's done," Rodney pressed.

"Which one? The ass slapping? No. Not happening." Bryan stared at his shoes. I watched the clench of his jaw, the red of his ears.

"No, forget that." Rodney waved his hand in the air, dismissive. "Do you like her? And don't fucking ask who. Severin, do you like her?"

I let the curtain slip from my hands. I didn't want to see his face when he answered. Because I knew the answer. It wasn't the one I dreamt about. The one I wrote about. The one I heard him say in our fictionalized story. It was the one I knew he would say in our reality. I closed my eyes as the words hit my ears.

"Of course I don't."

OFF LIMITS

THERE IS AN ART TO BETRAYAL. I'VE SEEN IT PAINTED before. Britt doesn't have it in her. She acts out of hurt, or a desire to say the right thing to fulfill a need. I'm still not sure which.

I just know my old best friend and my old enemy look thick as thieves. And who's to say it wouldn't slither into my friendship with Britt? Not that we had much of one anymore, anyway. And could she be friends with both of us? Maybe. Or perhaps I was just naïve.

To steal my best friend is to get revenge. To pull my secrets from her is to win. Something Aurora loves to do. And I deserve it. Don't I?

My art is mine. I can take my past and do whatever I wish with it.

I just forgot that there are consequences to my actions, to my words, and the way my stories are told.

I can't control who consumes them, how they are taken.

I can only control what I put out there. What I let spill. It will always be all of it. If not me, who would tell my life stories? I can survive the fallout. I will. I'm stronger than this petty leaking.

If I keep telling myself this, maybe it will be true.

I wave at Britt, stealing a moment when Aurora looks away, and my old friend's eyes are on me. She smiles, timidly, and nods her head toward a tree. "Hey, I just saw an old friend. I'll catch up with you later." I don't wait for Ben's answer, abandoning him quickly. An act I'm far too good at.

When I reach the tall oak Britt is standing under my neck flushes hot. Why do I feel like I'm involved in a clandestine meeting with a lover? Why does it feel like I'm doing something wrong? I always yield to Aurora. That's the answer I'm afraid to admit, but I'm getting closer.

"Hey!" My voice is too enthusiastic. It comes out squeaky and wrong. Britt is the one friend I never kept in touch with. The wound was too raw, her hurt too palpable. We all suffered a loss, but hers was the deepest. Her connection was the closest.

"Hi." She closes the space, reaches for me, and the hug is full body. I feel her in my toes, all the secrets we shared, all the gossip and the planning. I've missed her. "I didn't know you were coming back," she says.

I'm hard to track down. I have few family connections in town. I don't have a personal Facebook account anyone can find. Just one under my middle and last name set up to manage my public writing page. I shut down my original profile, created when Facebook was just a way for college kids to connect, ages ago. My phone number isn't even the same. I enjoy being a ghost. I enjoy knowing my past can't find me.

Britt pulls away and stares into my eyes. She shakes her head, and I reach for her hand. "What was that?"

"Did I see you over there with Ben Winthrop?"

"Yes. But the more pertinent question is, did I see you over there with Aurora...Winthrop?" I've never said it out loud. Her married name. The one I scribbled into notebooks, attached to mine.

"Yes. It's weird, right? Weird for you to see?" She scrunches up her nose, and her eyes squint. It's such an awkward face, and I do not know what to do with mine in return.

"I feel like I'm back in Mayberry. I'm surprised I don't see everything in black and white. And Bryan is working on the school across from my house. He was the first person I saw besides my dad and my aunt and sister. And now you're here with her. You're friends with her." I'm babbling. The Bryan admission, that I've seen him, slips out. Because standing in front of me is a lifeline. One of my dearest confidants. And it feels familiar. I realize my error too late. "I can't bring him up in front of you, can I?"

"Bryan?"

I cock my head to the side when she says his name. "Who else?" I don't mean to bite, but it's there. The *no shit* implication hovers between us.

"It would make me uncomfortable." She looks over in the direction she came from. I wonder if Aurora is watching us. I don't look.

"We used to talk about him all the time."

"Don't make me keep something from someone. Don't put me in that position." From a hello, to a hug, to this.

"In what position? The position of being my friend?" Everything is escalating. Britt and I never cared much for small talk. That was our thing. We always cut to the chase, spilled everything to each other.

"She's my friend, too, Severin. And you've been gone. You left me when I needed you." I look at the freckle on her jaw. Her hair is longer than it ever was in school. I can feel her energy. Resentment. Deserved.

"I went to college. It's not like it was some spur-of-the-moment thing." A lie. A boldfaced lie in the face of one of my closest childhood friends.

"That was never the plan. We were going to spend the summer together, the four of us. We made plans."

"It wouldn't have been the four of us even if I had stayed." I let that sit there, heavy. When she doesn't speak, when the silence between us becomes unbearable, I push her further. I make myself ugly, and I wish I could take it back before the words even fall. "I had to go. And if this is all you've accomplished, somehow becoming BFFs with Aurora, then maybe you should have left while you had a chance, too."

I walk away, a coward, before she can respond.

———

The heat is unbearable as I wander, avoiding eye contact. The heat, the gossip, they were parts of this town all on their own.

Yet, everyone is smiling, walking the square, visiting booths, laughing.

I startle at a man behind me, yelling, "Fresh funnel cake!"

Why would anyone want to eat hot funnel cake in this weather?

I walk away, deeper into the crowd. The hair prickles on my arms and I turn around, finding no one there.

This is one of my favorite memories. Running around with my friends, exploring the town. I knew every face back then, every name. I knew who was connected to who. Who I would see in the halls, who I would see dropping their kids off in front of the school.

I wasn't sure if I missed it or not. LA was so impersonal. I knew no one. I stepped out my door each day into an unknown. It was an escape I relished, an escape I needed.

I start toward the courthouse, centered in the middle of our small town. The sound of a fiddle pulls me, so I stop at the edge of a crowd, unable to see into the center in my worn flat sandals.

My peripheral vision catches a slight movement, something that generally wouldn't have caused me to look to the side, but I know the movement.

It's strange how our mind catalogs things, slight dances of movement. The way someone brings a glass of water to their lips.

This walk, I knew it. I knew the way he talked, the way he breathed.

My eyes catch Bryan's, and he smiles. That shy one, the one I wished was just for me, but I could never be sure.

He flicks his jaw, walks away. So, I follow. It's what I do with him. I want to be a different woman, but I am not. I am weak for him. We all have that one.

At the edge of the festival, he stands under a tall walnut tree. The biggest tree in town. There is a rusty swing set under the lower branches. My feet pull me to it. I grab the red chain and immediately drag my hand back, rubbing the flaky dust on my jean shorts.

"I reckon you'd probably need a tetanus shot if you swung on that. I don't even know why it's still here."

"Nostalgia?"

"Maybe." He shrugs.

The heat is more bearable here. I bend my knees, drop to the ground. I need to rest. The summer sun has zapped most of my energy. The heat is everywhere.

Bryan sits down beside me, close. I feel the sleeve of his shirt brush my bare shoulder. Leaning into him isn't an option. Just being seen with him is a risk. A risk for him, a desire for me.

"Did you need to ask me something?" I want to push him. To get a glimpse inside his head.

"No. I just wanted to be near you." His answer takes the breath from me.

I hide my fluttering heart. I don't let myself stammer. "I'm right here. This is a pretty public place. You sure you can be doing this? Your wife is here."

"I'm single, basically."

"You're not available." There's a difference. He knows this. "You never have been."

"That's not true."

"You've always been off limits." Even when he let me touch him, kiss him, run my hands over his hard lines. I felt it. The way I could never reach inside of him. I could never plant myself there. She was inside. From the beginning. There was only room for one.

"Maybe that's why you like me?" I like this tone. The bite from earlier is gone.

I laugh. "No. I'm not one of those girls. I've always wanted you, maybe I didn't always know why. Maybe I don't know why now. But I've always wanted you. And I've never once found it thrilling that you weren't mine. That everything we have ever done has been behind the scenes. In secret. Maybe some people get off on that kind of thing, but I don't. I want normal. I want someone who will take me on dates and someone who could walk me around that little town square with my hand in theirs. You've had that. I had that once, though it wasn't with anyone I truly loved. And it was a good feeling. No one should be kept away, a tryst. Someone to be ashamed of."

"I'm not ashamed of you."

"Bullshit." I think of the first time he made me feel small. Hidden behind a curtain, listening to him deny me.

"I don't know why I even came here." He buries his head in his hands. I'm jealous of those hands. I love his hair, his pale flesh. I want to touch him here. Pretend the town is vacant, that it's just the two of us.

When he is in my sight, I normally let my mind will everyone away in those ways. He is all I've cared for. All I've wanted to see. It was a slow disease, an unraveling.

My hand goes up, and I do not care who sees. His long fingers are soft under mine. He lets go of his hair, his heavy head, and turns to me.

Our hands drop to the grass and he lets me slip mine in between his. It's intimate.

"Want to get out of here?"

DON'T BREAK HER

PAST

I<small>T'D</small> B<small>EEN</small> A W<small>EEK</small> S<small>INCE</small> H<small>IS</small> C<small>RUSHING</small> W<small>ORDS</small>. S<small>INCE</small> his stake in my heart.

I don't stare at Bryan in class. I don't look at him in the hallways. I wasn't sure why I punished him. He didn't like me. That was fine. He wasn't obligated to want me just because I wanted him. But my humiliation fed me, festered in my belly. I could hear Rodney's words, his laughing voice. The entire school knew I was in love with Bryan and now I had to walk across a stage with him. I had to put on a dress, fix my hair, make myself vulnerable. The entire school would see through me, see my want and the way he flushed my skin.

I regretted our scheming, our plans. I regretted it all. But, save for a life-threatening illness, I was stuck doing this. I had to suck it up and figure out how to walk in heels. How to shut out the noise of a thousand teenagers. I had exhausted my friends with my worries, but they loved me. They indulged me. I left out Rodney's dumb ass plan for me. His words for me. I should have told them so Christina could really hear what kind of guy he was. Maybe it would have saved her.

It was a Friday night, and Britt, Akia, Christina, and I were cruising around our small town. There wasn't much to do, and we didn't party. So we drove in a loop, around the square, down by Al's Liquor, across the Town and Country parking lot. We turned the heat up and rolled the windows down. There were warm days, and there were biting cold days. Mother nature couldn't figure out which seasons she wanted to cling to.

Britt's car was a four-door Civic. It was perfect for us, and she was the only one able to drive in our group. When we became friends, we must have somehow known that we collectively had the strictest and most worrisome parents in Burlingame. Their tight reins had to account for some of our social standing at school.

The Nelly song we had been rapping came to an end, so I pushed forward in my seat, sticking my head between Britt and Christina. "Can we get back to the matter at hand now?"

Christina groaned. "You need to calm down. You have the perfect dress and Akia is going to do your hair."

Akia, seated next to me, reached up and squeezed my shoulder. "Yes. It's going to look great."

Britt chimed in, equally exhausted with me. "And tomorrow we are going to Topeka to get your shoes."

"I just want to get laid, and stop talking about your damn outfit and the fact that you get to walk in with your crush." Christina groaned.

I turned to her and made a mocking disgusted face. "You're a lady. Don't say things such as that." I imagined her losing her virginity to Rodney and shivered.

"I'll say as such as I want to." She stuck her tongue out at me.

"That didn't make sense."

"Your face doesn't make sense."

I bit Christina's shoulder, and she smacked me on the head. I fell back into my seat and kicked the back of hers. She'd distracted me. It always worked. She was my best friend, the best of the three, but her best friend was Britt. Akia was independent, she didn't need one of us to cling to, she stuck to us equally. I couldn't have survived a single day of school without them, and here we were, winding down. Reaching the end. We were in the back half of our senior year, and that terrified me. The knowledge that one day, soon, we wouldn't be in each other's lives every day, filled me with a sense of sadness I couldn't name. I pushed it away.

"You know those movies where friends make a pact to lose their V-card on prom night? Wouldn't that be fun?" I'm baiting them. I laugh silently and bite my lip.

"Gross," Britt scoffs from the front seat. "First of all, don't say 'V-card'. Second, only one of us has a damn prom date so far, and it's hard enough picking someone you think will look cute standing next to you that your parents will immortalize forever. Can you imagine hoping the person who asks you will also be someone you'll look back fondly on when you remember losing your virginity?"

"Do you think most people think much about it, though? Like, is some thirty-year-old woman sitting in yoga class randomly thinking about the night she lost her virginity? Maybe we are making too big a deal out of it," Akia said.

"I don't think we are." Christina stuck her hand out the window, moving it up and down like a bird in the night breeze. "I'm just not ready."

I wasn't ready either. There was only one person I could fathom giving myself to, and he had clearly declared his dislike for me romantically. I couldn't even look at him now, I was further from him than I had ever been. "I'm not either," I offered. "I could be. For the first person, it wouldn't even have to be love. Because I clearly have no idea what that is."

"None of us do. Maybe that's why we're here." Britt motioned around the car.

"What's love got to do with it?" Akia questioned, causing Britt and Christina to burst into song, doing their best Tina Turner impressions.

"This is why we are virgins." I laughed. We continued on like that for another half hour, finally deciding to park in the Town and Country grocery store parking lot. Britt popped her trunk and pulled two lawn chairs out. Christina grabbed one quickly, so Akia and I were left with the asphalt. We made a move to sit on it, but Britt motioned with her hands for us to stop. She pulled a blanket from the trunk and threw it at me. I wondered what else she had in there. The answer was Fireball. We huddled around the trunk and took a shot. It was my first.

"Do you have another blanket? It's getting chilly," I said, walking away from the trunk, shaking my head. I started gathering Akia's hair in my hands when she walked over to me. She loved when I put it in French braids. It was something my sister did for me when I was little. Britt started rifling through her trunk again, finding a soft pink blanket, then throwing it in our direction. It hit Akia in the face, making me laugh. "Ass."

Cars and trucks pulled in and out of the Town and Country parking lot while we watched. It was at the end of the small cruise loop. We could see every one of our classmates who were in town from this vantage point.

"Do you think we will become maybe, perhaps, sort of popular now that one of us has a car and we can see what everyone is doing?" Christina mused.

"No." Britt squashed her hope. "Senior year is almost over. This isn't a time for miracles."

"Bullshit," Akia countered. "We've pulled off three miracles. And if luck stays on our side, prom will be ours, too. Maybe we won't be losing our virginities but Christina you're going to be Prom Queen. I know it."

"I don't know. I think I'm going to be the failure of the bunch." She leaned back, her long hair fanning over Britt's trunk, right behind her seat.

"No," I replied, firm. "You're going to get it. I have a good feeling about this."

"You always have a good feeling about things when it doesn't involve you."

"I'm positive in your abilities to conquer, just not my own." I smiled. "Isn't that normal though? We can never have the same confidence in ourselves that we have in our friends and family."

"Truth," Akia confirmed.

"Okay. I'll take your word for it. Let's just focus on homecoming. Shit, speaking of..." Britt trailed off as a large black and gray truck pulled into the Town and Country parking lot. Instead of looping back out, Bryan's truck drove past us, to the back of the parking lot. It was dark back there. The street light that generally illuminated the back entrance had been out for months.

I dropped Akia's hair, and it unraveled in front of me. "What's he doing back there?" I whispered, even though there was no way he could hear me.

All three of my friends shrugged their shoulders in unison. None of us spoke then, our ears open. We saw him park, our eyes shooting fleeting glances in his direction. His engine died, then his truck door squeaked open.

"He's coming this way," Britt hissed. The sound of Bryan's truck door closing punctuated her sentence. Britt and Christina were facing his direction. I watched their faces, trying to read every move there. I heard his signature Nikes on the asphalt behind me. I couldn't ignore it, couldn't pretend I didn't hear it. I twisted at the waist, turning to him, my eyes traveling up his legs, up his long torso, to his eyes.

One hand was in his pocket, the other hand was on his face, his thumb pinched his lip. His eyes were dark, and his forehead was wrinkled. He looked pained, nervous. "Hey." His eyes were on mine, then flittering to my friends. "Hi, guys."

My friends murmured hellos, and I pushed off the ground, found my way to my feet somehow. "Hi."

"Can you come for a ride?" He jerked his head in the direction of his truck.

"Me?" I pointed to my chest, hearing Britt clear her throat behind me. *God, what an idiot. Yes, me.* "Yeah. I can."

Bryan nodded then looked at my friends. "I can take her home when we're done." I started to walk away, then turned around, patting my jeans, making sure I had my house key. I mouthed *'what the fuck?'* to Christina, taking in the color of her face.

"When you're done doing what, Winthrop?" Britt's voice was strong, confident.

I heard Bryan stop behind me. "Talking. I just want to talk to her."

"Don't break her," she replied and I eyed her hard.

"I wouldn't think of it," he replied, his hand on my elbow.

CROSS THE DISTANCE

Johnson's swimming hole is three miles out on the highway. Just past Miss Clara's house, my kindergarten teacher.

You take a left on the dirt road right by her house and follow it for two miles, then take a right on Dry Hollow Road.

The dust kicks up, leaving a billowing trail behind my car.

I'm sweating. Sweating everywhere. My thighs are stuck to the leather seats, I can just tell. And I can't stop obsessing over the sound it will make when I get up, out of this vehicle. I don't want the drive to end. For many reasons.

I do that—obsess. And the object of my deepest, longest, most painful obsession is driving me to a spot everyone in high school knew was reserved for make-outs, skinny dipping, and sex, at least back in the day.

I'm game for all those things. I'm not the shy little virgin he took down this dirt road over ten years ago.

He doesn't have a powerful advantage over me anymore.

I study his arm, gripping my steering wheel, his clenched jaw. He said he wanted to drive, so I had tossed him my keys. I do not turn away now, not like before.

He doesn't turn to me when he speaks. "What are you looking at?"

"You. You, in all your confusion, over me. It's kind of hot."

"Shut up."

"Must suck to not have me under your thumb. To not have me panting for you, adoring you. Must suck to not have it all. Does the golden boy even know how to live like that?"

"I've been living like that for a while. There is nothing golden about me." He sounds weary, worn from life. His skin is wrinkled around the eyes. Maybe more from the sun than smiles.

"I'm aware. My mind stripped you of that a while ago. Everything here looks different. Dirtier, smaller." He looks more beautiful, bigger, but I don't give him that.

"Must be nice to be so high and mighty," he says, giving it back. My smugness.

"This is exhausting." I cross my arms as he turns.

"What is? Fighting with me?"

"Sparring with you," I correct him. "Sparring with your brother. All of it." I barely sparred with Ben. But it was enough to get under my skin.

"You've been fighting with my brother?" He ignores my word for it. My guess is he doesn't know the difference. What a shame.

"For a minute there. We walked around town for a bit. I don't have any friends here." I think of my weird encounter with Britt. "It was nice to see a face happy-ish to see me."

"I see." His jaw clenches.

"What is it with you and your brother?" I've never been able to figure it out. To figure them out.

"He bugs me."

"You bug me." I roll my eyes at myself when Bryan puts my car in park. I barely have time to look at him before he is out the door, slamming it behind him.

I follow. *Why do I follow so willingly?*

The creek is low. I can see where the water was up, high, ripping away the surrounding rocks. April had been heavy with rain. My aunt told me it was a record high.

All of that is gone, the water that tore it all up. Just wreckage lingers behind. Leaves are stuck in low hanging branches.

Bryan is staring across the creek. Three milk cows stand by a barbed wire fence, eyeing us. I eye them back.

"You got beef with that cow over there?" I laugh to myself.

"Was that supposed to be a funny joke?"

"I mean, I laughed." I shrug my shoulders. I have a tendency to make jokes when I'm nervous. Or when there is a silence to fill.

"It's a dairy cow."

"I know. I just thought I would milk this moment for all it's worth." I bite my lip to hide the laugh.

"This is why you weren't popular in school."

I shove him, and he stumbles, his smile meets my glaring face when he turns back.

"Why are we here?" I whirl around, stare up into the trees.

"Do you ever feel like everyone is watching you?"

"No. Paranoid much?"

"Just, Burlingame. Everyone watches you there. You can't do a damn thing without the whole town knowing. And talking about it. And judging you for it."

"Oh, that. Yeah. I guess I don't care. I didn't care all that much in school, and I don't care now. I won't be sticking around, so..."

"Must be nice. I have to live with it. Everything I do. Everything I say. It's out there. I'll never live anything down. I'll never have a moment of peace." The pressure on him is stifling. I've seen him shudder under it. I've seen it make him a coward.

"But it's always been that way. You're not used to it yet? Just, get over it. Stop being such a baby. So some old bitty at the diner wants to gossip about your marriage, so what?" I'm testing boundaries. Testing my language with him. I don't know where we will go with this. What version of me I will be in his presence.

"They'll talk about you, too. That doesn't bother you?"

"I mean, I'm not inhuman. Maybe it's bothered me at some point, more than I want to admit. In high school, I didn't like the way everyone gossiped. But I had my friends. We lived in our own little bubble, and we helped each other not care. Didn't you have that? You had tons of friends."

"I had tons of people I hung out with. There's a difference." He won't look me in the eyes.

"Whatever. You had so many friends." I dismiss his dramatics. Dismiss thoughts of his nameless friend. I will not speak of him.

"No. Not anyone I was really close with."

"Aurora?"

"Yeah. I was closest with her."

"Marriage is weird. Aren't you supposed to be best friends with your spouse?" I imagine my mother and father were just that. Beautiful and sepia, like an old movie.

"What a crock. My parents weren't. Yours?"

"Maybe. I don't know." It's the truth. I make up so many realities for them. I write stories they will star in. Because my parents will never star in another scene in this life.

"I sometimes wonder if mine were, before. Before he drank all the time. Before me. They were high school sweethearts, you know? So there had to have been a time when they were best friends. When they talked, and they cared about each other. Aurora's parents were high school sweethearts, too. Our parents were best friends in school. Our moms and our dads. It's like, we had no choice but to end up together."

"That's cute." I make my tone mocking to hide my curiosity. I want to zero in on the slip of the tongue. Before he drank? Pastor Winthrop?

"Shut up."

"I'm not being snarky this time. I mean it. Looking at it from the outside. Yes, it's cute. I wish it had worked out." Maybe I do. Maybe

I don't. I want to run out of town, leave this train wreck. Everything I left behind is just as it was before. We have now just resumed. It's unsettling.

"And now you're lying."

"No. I can want two separate things. I wanted you before. But now I just want you to be happy, I guess." I shrug my shoulders and try to figure out if I'm lying. I don't even know.

"You guess?" He laughs. I like to see him laugh. It reminds me of the past. "Well, if you want me to be happy, then don't want me to be with Aurora. Those two things don't go hand in hand."

"You overcomplicate everything, you know?" He did before, and he is now. We are a strange gravity. Maybe there is something to it. Maybe I can have him this time.

"I did. I overcomplicated my life, and now it is what it is. There is no changing this. This is my bed. I gotta lie in it."

"So dramatic. I swear." I pop my neck, draw his eye there.

"I miss your accent. You don't talk like us anymore." He turns fully, walks toward me.

I back away. I don't bring up the fact that his brother said something similar. Instead, I walk to the water, slip my flip-flops off. It feels so cool, it cools the blush on my cheeks, the one I need to hide from him. "It's not like we have strong accents here. Everyone I meet can hear it."

"Maybe. But you sound different."

"You're just not used to hearing me talk this much. That's what it is." I bit my tongue so much back then. I wanted to make sure every word was one he liked. One that would help me win him. And I lost.

"Maybe. I wish you would have spoken up more back then."

"Would you have listened?" I turn back to him. To his crossed arms, sharp jaw. He shakes his head.

"Let's call it what it is." His voice is hushed. He was not like this ten years ago. "I peaked in high school. I was popular, and I got the girls I wanted, and I took the team to state, and I passed, at least. But I didn't have dreams. I knew I had to make the most of it then. I knew I wasn't getting out. Maybe that's why I was drawn to you then. I could see it in you. You were meant for more. You were going to make more of yourself than this. You were going to leave. And you did. I wish you hadn't been forced to come back. This can't be anything you wanted."

"My father? Of course not."

"And to be tangled back into something with me. I know I am assuming, but I feel some sort of energy between us. Like there was never a moment you were gone from here. Do you feel it?"

I nod.

"This can't be anything." He motions between us. "We can't start back up. We can't be a thing."

"I know it can't." I'm pissed at him for assuming, though he may be right. "I knew it then, and I know it now. I've never dreamed of more for us," I lie. "I've always known it was moments. Laced together. Fleeting."

He groans, walks toward me. I move to the side, hoping he is just reaching for the riverbed, wanting to place his feet in the creek, too. To cool himself off. He looks across the water, smiles. "I just love the way you talk. I always have. I've never understood why you wanted me. Besides the obvious. I'm just a fucking idiot, really."

"You're not. Stop saying that." I miss the confident Bryan. It was his silent air and those confident secret smiles that pulled me in.

"Why not? You graded my tests, you talked to me back then. Empty words and bullshit charm, that's all I am. It's what my father was, my brother, all of us. We have that skill."

"Quit crying, okay? Quit bitching." I'm over his pity party. Over his excuses. I want to shake him from it.

"Wow, okay."

"Isn't this my job? To ruin everything with words?"

"Yeah," he laughs, "I guess it is."

I think of their daughter together. What am I doing here? I was trying to wedge my way in between again. Where I didn't belong but where I so desperately wanted to be. I didn't think long dead feelings could be resurrected like this. They had over ten years together. A last name. Families that had become one.

I felt like an only child for a big chunk of my childhood. I grew up with one parent. I didn't know this. Their intimacy.

Once, maybe, for a few years, my ex and I possessed something similar. I push away thoughts of him. Thoughts of who I made myself with him. I lost my bite with him. I lost my sass and every part of myself I built up after high school.

"I think it's normal," I start, "to feel a little lost in life. It's okay that you feel this way. I've felt that way. I feel that way now. But we have to decide what we are doing here."

"Here?" He spreads his arms wide, glancing around the field. The headlights of my car set him on fire. The sun is nearly down.

"No." I laugh. "Here, in this part of our lives. On this course. Whatever it is, it has to have a purpose. If you feel you haven't been living a purposeful life, then change it. Change your mind about yourself."

"I don't know if I can. This is it for me. This small town and this small life."

"And you won't leave, right?" I know the answer. He doesn't give himself enough credit. He loves his daughter, like any good father should. It doesn't matter what is going on with his wife, with me. With his dreams and the plans he had. He cannot abandon her. And I respect him for that.

When I was a young girl, I desired him. I needed him to look at me. To pick me. But he was never someone I respected. Back then, I thought respect was something you only handed out to your parents, your teachers, people older than you.

"No, I can't leave. I don't want to. I mean, I want to, but no. She's here and I'll never leave her." He squints his eyes across the creek bed.

I know he's talking about his daughter, but my breath hitches. I think of Aurora.

He won't leave her either. This is torture, and I'm not sure if this is love, the way my skin itches and I feel burned from the inside, but when I was eighteen I thought that's what it was when he kissed me for the first time in front of the entire school.

I thought, *this is what romance is. This is what movies have. This is the beginning of a story you tell your kids.*

I thought it for long nights when I was in bed. When other kids were out drinking, having fun, having sex, I was clinging to this fantasy of him. Of what we could only be in my mind. I walk over to him, he turns at the sound of my feet on the gravel. I reach for his hand, and he lets me take it. His long slender fingers intertwine with mine, and I feel like I'm falling backward, deep into the past. My other hand reaches, crashes into his, the one already reaching for me. I let my head fall to his chest, his jaw finds my hair. I'm humming and hungry. I'm alive, so very alive. "I can't believe I get to touch you again." I clench my eyes, half hoping he doesn't hear me.

"Stop," he says. "I'm nothing worth...I'm nothing."

"And we will do this dance until we die maybe. No, until I leave." I disconnect. I pull away and cover my chest with my arms, defensive and half laughing. The vulnerability shaking me.

"When will you leave?" He mirrors my stance.

"When the house is finished, cleaned up. When it's ready to be put on the market. My last little tie to this place." We start tomorrow, my aunt and sister and me. Even if my father gets better, it will fade. He will fade back into the dark. He will never live in his own home again. He will never be able to care for himself again.

"And I'll fade away again? Right?" Fade. It's as though he has plucked the words from my mind. I shake my head, my laugh now silent, tired.

"As if I didn't do that for you, too?" I pull the hair tie from my wrist, begin gathering my long honey hair at the nape. His eyes map my neck. I drop my hands to my sides when I'm done, inch closer to him.

"Maybe you did. Maybe for a few years. Then you would pop into my head. Sometimes I would resent you. Sometimes I would fanta-size about the other path I could have taken. Sometimes I would remember being down by the water with you. The color of your shirt. It was baby blue."

I pull my eyes from the trees, cross the distance. My lips take his and I'm not ashamed. I want to feel his desire. His fleeting regrets and his hands, anywhere he will put them.

His hair is soft under my fingers, shorn close to his head, autumn brown and not long enough for me to pull. I desperately want to make him hurt a little. Just a little, something to match the ache he always pours into my chest with that voice of his.

I feel my back hit the side of a tree. My legs go up, around.

We have too much on. The air is still hot. Summer won't let go and neither will I.

His tongue traces my collarbone, I clench my eyes.

"Fuck me." I want to say *fuck you, fuck you for all you do to me. This crush and the crushing weight of your beauty.*

But I don't. I tell him what I want. Finally. So many years unfulfilled stretch between us. I want to close the distance on them.

MIRROR ME

PAST

THE AIR DOWN BY THE CREEK WAS COOL. I HAD goosebumps along my arm. My baby blue top was low, my breasts swelled, my breathing sped up. I pulled my jean jacket closed.

I didn't know what he expected. Our experience levels, they couldn't be the same. No way was he a virgin like me. Not with the way he and Kelsey Cooper hung all over each other in the hall our junior year.

I cleared my throat, grabbed a rock from the bridge surface. I used to skip rocks with my sister and father when I was a little girl. I was good at it, better than them, and they were the ones who taught me.

"How are you?" He picked up a rock, tried to mimic my throw. It was off. I was better at something than he was. Something other than English, poetry, and French.

"I'm okay." I wasn't okay. Homecoming was fast approaching. I was in love with the boy next to me, and he had made it clear to his friends he didn't even like me. Now I was alone with him and feeling warm, despite the weather. I had taken my first shot and found myself somewhere I never expected. "What do you need to talk to me about?"

He cleared his throat, gave up the rock skipping. His hands went to his pockets, and he rocked on his heels. "I'm sure you've heard some of my friends talking about homecoming. I know they have been going on about it in the halls, and we go to a small school, so, yeah." His voice was hurried, nervous. It was refreshing. To see him mirror me and my past behavior.

I skipped one more rock, then dusted my hands on my thighs.

"You mean you want to know if I've heard how they want you to slap my ass if I win?" It was juvenile, even for his crew. I was no longer bothered by it. Not that part. I looked at Bryan and he nodded, remaining silent. "And how exactly would you *be my daddy?*" I turned to him fully, half rolled my eyes. "That doesn't even make sense. I'm not surprised the idea came from Rodney. He's a prick, and he can't spell for shit." I hated Rodney. More now than ever.

"He's an idiot. And unoriginal." Bryan smiled, his shoulders, once tense going slack.

"Don't worry about it."

"But I have been."

"Why? Why are we here?" I wanted the point. I wanted something from him. I wanted to reach out, take his hand, press it to my lips. I was nothing but wanting and whining and wounds.

"I wanted you to know I absolutely won't do that if you win."

I laughed, walked to the edge of the bridge. I lowered myself down and swung my legs over the side. The water was down, so my feet would stay dry. I heard Bryan follow. "You and I both know I won't win. It would upset the delicate balance of the high school hierarchy." My tone was mocking, thick to hide my fears and insecurities.

"But isn't that exactly what you've done already? You and your friends?" He sounded impressed. I was sure his friends did not feel the same. Their dirty looks were proof enough. Someone had slipped little pieces of paper in all our lockers. One word was written on them. *Fakes.*

"I guess we have. Does that bother you?" I wanted to know exactly how he felt. I could give two shits about his tired ass crew.

"No. It bothers my friends, though," he replied, confirming my suspicions.

"Are you a lemming?" I was forward. I blamed the shot. I blamed the night. I blamed the ticking in my head. The reminder that our time was winding down.

"No." He sounded sure, but I doubted his inner voice was confident in his defiance. Would he answer the same way if they were here? I knew the truth. It made me ashamed of my want for him.

"I'm glad you're nice enough to go with not humiliating me in front of the whole school. Five gold stars." I punched him in the arm, the way you would a sibling, or a friend. I wanted to slap myself across my own face. *God. Sexy, Sev.*

"Thanks." He laughed, rubbing his arm. "Are you nervous for next week?"

"You have no idea." I wanted it to be over. I wanted graduation to be here. I wanted out of here. We made senior year harder than it needed to be, adding these games to the mix. "I feel like I'm walking around, holding a breath, just floating or something. Do you ever feel that way?"

"Every day." His voice was melancholy and I had never heard him speak that way.

"But your life is perfect."

He blew out a breath at the last word. Shook his head.

My mind flashed through all the things he had. His beautiful smile and his friends and his family and their beautiful home.

"It's not. Not even close."

"You're the most popular guy in school. Your parents are perfect. Your grades aren't perfect, but that's fine. Everything is fine and not on fire in your life. You're like, floating on a cloud of fine." He laughed at my rambles.

"Don't you think there is someone at school, one of the really unpopular girls, maybe, or someone with no friends? Don't you think someone is looking at you, thinking *she has it all* when she sees you laughing with your friends? Because you four seem to always be laughing. And you have each other's backs. It's rare, right? To have that kind of group. To look at a group of friends and know they just get each other. I see more than you would guess."

"Honestly, that doesn't surprise me. You seeing things. You're taciturn. It's what made me notice you. But what does surprise me, is you noticing us at all."

"I noticed you, they're just part of the deal."

"Wow." I don't hide the words. I let him see me smile and blush. "What else do you see?"

"Sometimes I'll watch you and your dad in church on Sundays."

"What do you see there?"

"Something a lot of people don't have."

"Something you don't have?" I don't know much about his family. Just that they appear to be perfect. And I know nothing is perfect. His mother is tall, slender, beautiful. She is quiet, unlike her husband, whose voice pierces the church. It's never been a voice I liked. The tone was unsettling. I thought maybe, if someone else were preaching, I would want to know more about God. I wasn't sure if my father went to church before he met my mother. But one memory I do have of her is her hand in mine on Sundays. Of her voice when she sang in the pew next to me. My father would get out of church during football season. And when she was gone, he didn't have anyone to butter up for the grace. We all stayed home in the fall. My father watched the games and I read on the couch. I would never have those moments again.

"Yeah. Something I don't have," Bryan replied.

"I didn't notice," I murmured. I had fallen for the ruse. The fantasy.

"I can hide things better than most. It's part of the deal."

CROCK OF SHIT

I'M RIDING A HIGH WHEN MY SISTER WAKES ME UP THE next morning. A high I need, to make it through this. Without my rock in on my secrets, I'm wavering. And my wounds, I fear, will be on full display.

I wanted nothing more than to be like Sasha when I was younger. She was popular. Beautiful. She wore the kind of intelligence she never had to pay for. My own grades were passable, but nothing to rave about. She spoke to adults like she was an adult, so they responded in kind.

Sasha always seemed capable. Often times the oldest child suffered with the strictest rules, and when the second child came along everything was more lenient.

That wasn't the case in our home. Sasha could handle any task you threw at her. With me, it was questionable. When we wanted something from the store, our father would give us some cash, tell us to check out ourselves. I always froze, changed my mind about the item I thought I needed.

Simple things terrified me. I was painfully shy back then.

I avoided answering the phone at home. What if it was a telemarketer? I was so painfully awkward I may let them convince themselves they were close to selling me a time-share. I didn't know when to say no. When or how to exit gracefully. It would take some time to grow out of that.

I put off learning to drive until the beginning of my senior year. I could see the entrance to my high school from my bedroom window. Later, I let Britt drive me everywhere. It all fit into my plan to avoid going behind the wheel as long as possible.

My mother had been the artist. Sasha and I had inherited our interests from her. Or maybe, my sister inherited her love for the arts from our mother, and I just wanted to be like my big sister, ten years older than me.

When Sasha moved to New York for college, I knew I would do the same. I knew I would have to follow her, to escape our small town as well.

It was scary, but knowing I would be moving to a big city where the person I looked up to the most lived made it a little easier to swallow.

Sasha's girlfriend was a Director of Theater Development on Broadway.

When I arrived in the city over ten years ago, heartbroken and terrified of the noise and movement around me, they took me in.

They taught me how to use the subway system. How to get to and from class quickly.

They were my lifeline.

My sister had always been my idol. Living with her changed that. She became my best friend. My person. The one I told everything to.

I missed my father, but my sister was my home. I had missed her terribly since she left Burlingame after her graduation. Her visits weren't frequent enough. Airfare wasn't cheap, and city life was expensive.

The shock of it was almost too much at first when I escaped.

I stayed in my room studying for the most part of that first year. I couldn't afford to do much else, and I knew I had it easy, living rent-free.

Sasha was my escape route, always in the back of my mind. She was my biggest encourager. Any flame that burned inside of me, she fanned. Any battle I was facing, she would help me fight it.

But this battle that we were facing here, we could not win it.

We would lose our father. And we would never be the same.

We would be orphans.

Our mother was an only child. Our father had one sibling. We had no grandparents.

When our father was gone, we would never return to our hometown, to our old bedrooms. To any of this.

Life forces you to grow up when you least expect it. When you don't want it to. I knew that better than most. These streets reminded me of it. I had over ten years of chasing dreams, pretending my past was some story I had written in my journals.

I didn't know what it felt like to have an all-consuming love. I had a boyfriend in college, Johnson. We were together for two years. We broke up and I never let myself think about him, but maybe I did love him. Maybe.

Hell, I thought of Bryan more over the years than I did of anyone else.

But I did not confuse that for love when the sun was up. When I wasn't caught up in the lust of it all. It was something unfinished. And his presence hung around like an omen before I came back here, because of the play, then the movie. I wouldn't let his figure leave, this larger than life memory of him, this idea of him I carried with me all those years, it was fading. Now it was replaced with the scent of his skin on my own, the remembrance of his soft flesh.

I roll over and grab my phone from my old white wicker nightstand. When I flip it over, I see a text from my aunt telling me she will be here in forty-five minutes. She spent the night at her boyfriend's house in Topeka. I'm so happy she has someone in her life now. Someone to give her grief to.

I don't see a text from Bryan, and my stomach rumbles a little. I gave him my number last night after we slept together.

I don't know what I was expecting. A good morning text, or a text of regret. Anything would have been nice. Some tangible reminder that what happened last night was real. I pull my phone to my chest, lie back on my pillow, and close my eyes. I got little sleep. I feel loopy, like I'm floating above the comforter. The attic fan hums and I feel a missing for LA. I miss my air conditioning and the quiet solitude of my bedroom. I miss the familiar routine of my nights spent writing. When I hold so much in, when there is no outlet, I'm on edge.

There is no moment to write here. Every hour is full of new commitments. I pull the covers away again and swing my legs off the bed. I need a shower. And caffeine, but I won't allow myself. I won't allow myself to indulge. I look at my phone again and groan at the ominous number sitting over the email app.

I scroll, delete, reply, as I make my way to the small bathroom down the hall. My eye catches on Ben's name as I sit down to pee. I feel raw and open. My body isn't used to biting, bark on back, breathless moans. It's been a while since I've been thoroughly fucked. Bryan knew what he was doing. So why am I staring at an email from his brother with the subject heading *"Lunch?"*

I put my phone by the sink and pause. I need friends here. Community is important, and I've felt an emptiness in my chest since I left New York. LA has never fit me.

I wash my hands and pick my phone back up. I open the email and immediately smile. I can hear Ben's voice as I read the text. "Let's be friends and stuff," is all it says. It ends with his phone number. I'm impressed that he searched for my email. I like to see effort. I walk out of the bathroom, back into my old bedroom, to the window next to my bed. I stare at the school and wish I could be there. I wish I could ask Bryan what last night meant. This wasn't what I expected. To come into town and find his body close to mine. To hit the unpause button on a romance that has given me more ache than relief.

I text Ben a "hi" then lock my phone and toss it on the bed.

———

When my sister wakes up I'm caught. "Why do you look weird?" she says when she brings in a plate of pancakes and sits down on my floor. There is no hiding from her. My sister is an extension of me, though I've never been able to read her as well as she can me.

I shake my head at her and lie on my bed, let my feet dangle back and forth. She doesn't let me hide. "Tell me, Sev. Is it Dad? I'm sorry I wasn't here that first day. I know it was hard." She wants to protect me, always. I can hear it in her voice. She wants to be a shield for the world, and maybe that has made me soft in some ways.

"It was hard. I don't know how to say what's inside my chest. I'm glad you're here now." I hear her moving across the room. She puts her plate on my vanity, then lies on the bed next to me, intertwines her fingers in mine.

"We are going to make it through this." She is using her mom voice. The one that tries to hide any worry she may have.

"You're going to get me through this. Like always."

"You can stand on your own two feet, Sev. I know what you're thinking." She knows part of it.

"It's smaller here, and that hasn't made me feel less unsure of the world."

"Life is scary and bullshit and hard as hell. But we have to get up and face it. Have you had any stimulants?"

I laugh at her question. My anxious running mind is a product of my own worries, genetics, no outside source. "No."

"Well, something is going on in that head of yours. Something besides Dad. Tell me what it is quick because we need to go wash up and get up there to see him." She pushes off the bed, walks to my vanity, and inspects her eye makeup while grabbing her plate. When she's done, she turns, stares until I push off the bed as well.

I place my palms on my knees, take a deep breath. "I slept with Bryan Winthrop last night." I shake my head and tears fill my eyes. I wasn't expecting to be this overwhelmed. But in front of Sasha, I feel the tumble. I feel the familiar hum of her mothering figure. I had not realized how wound up I had been. She is looking at me so intently, full of awe and worry.

"Sev, are you serious?" She crosses the space between us, and embraces me. To quiet the tears that are now streaming down my face. I do not like to be this fragile. I prefer sarcasm and wit. I prefer the way I can ward off the vulnerability that comes with opening up. With everyone. With anyone but her. "What the fuck, why are you crying?" She is laughing in my hair, and it pulls a laugh from my throat. Something hysterical and garbled.

"I don't know." I pull away and wipe my eyes. "We just got here, and it's so strange to be here. I miss her, and I miss you, and I miss Dad, and he doesn't remember me. This isn't fair. Nothing is fair. Then I see Bryan, and he's working on the school across the street, and it's like nothing has changed. Except everything has. He and Aurora are separated, and this wall is down. This giant wall that was always between us. Not my shyness and his ridiculous popularity. Not imaginary walls. The whole town knows I'm here and they saw the movie, and they know. They know, and I don't know if I can be here. It's too much." My voice is shaky and unsure. I want the confidence back. The way I smirked at Bryan and the way I took control. I want that part of myself back.

"Sev, it's okay. You're freaking out over nothing." She wipes my cheeks.

"Nothing? I thought I loved him." I grab her hands.

"Yeah, you did think that. But you didn't." Our hands fall down, and she squeezes them.

"What do you mean I didn't?" I furrow my brow, take my hand away, and wipe my face.

"It was a high school crush. And he cheated on the girl he ended up marrying, with you. You know how preachers' kids are. They're the worst kind. So messed up and confused. That's all he ever has been. I remember every sad phone call you made when you were in high school. I remember the way he hurt you."

"Maybe it'll be different this time." It sounds like a crock of shit coming out of my mouth. I should write that feeling down, tattoo it to my damn eyeballs, but I push it aside.

My sister's voice is firm. "It's going to end badly, again."

Mine is hesitant. "You don't know that."

"Yes, I do. And so do you."

"So you're saying I should go have lunch with his brother, then?" I laugh through my tears and grab my phone.

DO THAT AGAIN

PAST

"I WANT YOU TO REMEMBER THIS, SEVERIN," MY FATHER said, on a Thursday night around nine. I was steaming my home-coming dress, lost in my thoughts and the feeling of nervousness that would overcome me the next day at school as I counted down the hours until the game and the ceremony. "No one should ever be put in the shadows." He was sitting at the kitchen table with the newspaper in front of him. He never got a chance to look at it in the morning so he always read it at night.

"What's that, Dad?" I had been half listening, half nodding and pretending. He had my attention now.

"Your mother, she had a serious boyfriend before we started dating. His name was Bart, so you know." He rolled his eyes and I laughed.

"Cassidy is a much better name," I said, smiling at my father.

"Yes. Much better. Anyway. She had this boyfriend, and I noticed them sometimes, but I had my head in my ass and you know, I was just an idiot kid. She had a crush on me because she saw me with my girlfriend at the time and I liked to hold her hand and I was affectionate. I was a gentleman. I took her on dates and your mother, she would see me on these dates when she was out with her girlfriends. Not with her boyfriend. Because he was always hanging with the boys. Never spending time with your mother. Never showing her off."

"Who wouldn't want to show Mom off?" I scoffed. My mother with the corn silk hair and long legs. My mother with the wide smile and dark eyes.

"An idiot, clearly. Anyway, she let it define her worth for a little too long there. When she and I started dating, finally, when I finally got my head out of my ass and realized she liked me, I showed her off. And it threw her. She knew I was that kind of guy. The kind that wanted his girl by his side, even when he was hanging with the guys, but she always worried she was taking up too much of my time. Because she was used to thinking she was taking up some-one's time just by being with them. And that is just silly. So, I want to know that when you get a boyfriend, you get the kind that will take you out and make you a priority."

"Okay, Dad." I laughed, but I was pushing it down, the fear. Bryan was never going to give me the time of day. And if he did, would he walk down the hall with his hand in mine? No way. It's a strange thing, to resent the object of your desire for faults you know they own, but have never confirmed. This crush was silly and I would give up sacred parts of myself for it. I knew it. It made me want to slap myself across the face. No matter what name was said tonight. No matter the victories my friends and I would achieve. Bryan Winthrop's heart would never be mine. Never in the light of day.

"Severin Thompson," my father said, pulling me from melancholy.

"Yes," I said, blinking twice.

"Your intuition is a powerful thing. You know when someone is doing you right. You know when you deserve more."

"Dad." I sighed. "I'm not even dating anyone. It's okay. Sasha was the big dater. You don't have to worry about me."

"Yes. She did date a lot. But I also noticed a lot. And I gave her these same talks. Talks she didn't understand at the time. Or, no, she understood. But we just didn't talk about it yet. What we both knew."

I thought of my sister. My sister who struggled as a teen with her preference for the female gender in a small town in the Midwest. I looked at my father and smiled. Oh, how I loved him. And he was right. I understood what he meant, and what he wanted me to know. He saw more than he let on.

"Severin Thompson," he repeated.

"Yes." I smiled, shaking my head.

"I love you. Good luck tomorrow."

"Thank you. I love you, too."

———

I couldn't hear anything the next night right after my name was announced as the new Homecoming Queen, not even my father's warning. There was a buzzing in my ears. Everything was slow motion, blurry. I stood in line, the head of the line. I saw a microphone in Erica's hand. I saw her lips moving, her smile. My hand was sweating, and I wondered if Bryan could sense it. He was pressed against me, warm. Close but not close enough. I hated that the whole school was seeing it. My first moments of being near him in this way.

Moments before, Bryan turned my way, just slightly, so I leaned in. Always falling.

"Are you okay?"

"*No.*" I mouthed it. No sound came out. He nodded, staring again. His hand came up, covering mine. He squeezed it gently, and I felt my heart rate speed up. That didn't help. He was here, by my side, in front of the whole school. I knew my father was in the crowd but he didn't know this was the one my heart wanted. This was the one I wanted and he was here with me, for everyone to see.

The stands erupted in cheers when the moment came. I didn't register what was happening. I saw flashing lights, Mandy Thornbury—yearbook photographer—came my way. I pulled my hand up, shielded my eyes. I registered Bryan moving away from me, turning.

I pulled my hand down and looked up into his eyes. A smile played on his lips, the half one that always made my stomach flip, the one he had shown me down by the water a week earlier, in secret.

Bryan's hand was now on my jaw, his thumb under the tip of my chin. My mouth opened slightly, a quick breath came out and then it was lost. His mouth was on mine, and it was not a peck. It was not over in a second. My eyes were closed, and I felt his tongue pressing against my lips, so I opened for him. His body pressed against mine and my hands, they moved up, slowly tracing his neck, feeling the beautiful vein I always found with my eyes when he spoke. I don't know how much time passed, but I knew one thing. This was a kiss. This wasn't for show. This wasn't for tradition. This was something he wanted and something he was giving me as more than a gift. It was something he needed to feel. The cheers got louder, then I felt cool air on my lips.

I blinked, pulled my hand up, traced my thumb over my bottom lip. It was wet, swollen. I felt dizzy and wanting.

Bryan wasn't looking at me when I opened my eyes. He was blushing, shaking his head.

Mandy's voice was close, an urgent murmuring. I turned to see her leaning toward us.

"Guys. I didn't get a picture. I need," she hesitated, then laughed a little, "I need you to do that again."

I shook my head. Not up and down or side to side, it was a mixture of both. I was a confused bobble head. I turned to Bryan, and this time his eyes were on me. He nodded, pursed his lips. "I think I can do that."

It was just as intense the second time. I felt hot all over, especially between my thighs. It wasn't a foreign feeling in his presence, but it was strange to feel this buzzed with his hands on me. It wasn't just a fantasy this time, something I made up.

When we pulled away again, I searched the crowd. His hand had mine, and I felt like an imposter. I found my friends in the crowd and shook my head from side to side, like a deranged idiot. Britt was pumping her hand in the air. Akia looked like she was crying. And Christina, she was pointing. I followed her index finger's direction and my breath caught. Aurora was at the edge of the basketball court. Her hands were over her mouth. She looked like she had just seen one of her family members get hit by a car. Her skin was as pale as her blonde hair, and I felt sick. I squeezed Bryan's hand, unintentionally, needing him to look into my eyes. To tell me I wouldn't be paying for this moment.

He ignored it, pulling me along. The yearbook staff arranged us with the rest of the candidates in the center of the gymnasium floor for more photos. I avoided Rodney's stare, but I could feel it. I avoided him completely. He hadn't won, and that felt good.

Strangely enough, Bryan's younger brother, a junior, Ben Winthrop won. For one photo they had us stand together, arms locked. He congratulated me, and I mumbled *"thanks"* or something to that effect.

Eventually, I noticed a change in Bryan's posture. I noticed the tightness of his hand in mine lessening until he let go completely.

When my palm hit my dress, I looked up into his eyes. They weren't looking at me anymore. They were looking across the gym at Aurora, who was now crying.

EVERYTHING IS A GAME

IT'S LIKE A GHOST TOWN AT HOURS LIKE THIS. I COULD scream into the night and a flurry of lights would flicker on. I don't, because I want the loneliness seeping into my bones. I want the sound of the cicadas, the winds whipping around me. An American flag thrashes around in the center of town, the sound violent and off-putting.

I take my shoes off when I meet the grass of the square. My pink toes are the color of the mood I wish to be in, but that's not going to happen. The day has been long and draining.

Earlier, before lunch, my father and I walked around the courtyard at the home. My father's hand was on my forearm. I could feel my sister's eyes burning into us. She wanted so much for him to have a good day. For him to call her by her name, not our mother's name. Not his sister's name. Not his own mother's name.

I didn't mind. He could call me what he wanted to, as long as he was smiling. I couldn't take the wailing again. I couldn't take his sad eyes. I needed his wisdom. His advice. I found my old notebook this morning, before we left for the home. It was filled with his small stories on life. His beautiful life, so well lived.

No one should ever be put in the shadows. I had run my fingers over his words, words I scribbled so long ago.

I thought of those words as my father held onto me this afternoon. We turned around at the edge of the grass, made our way back to my sister. She was frowning, her forehead creased. I shook my head at her, pulled the index finger of my free hand up to my mouth, drawing a smile there. She rewarded me with a fake smile that was more scary than comforting.

My sister is a sponge. She feeds off the emotions of others. I try to think happy thoughts. To even my breathing and look for the good in this day. I tried that today, hoping my father could feel it.

The good news was that my father was walking around. He wasn't talking much, and his cough has lessened, they say. The color of his skin wasn't as gray. There was a pink in his cheeks. The Kansas heat would do that to anyone. I was sweating in places I'd rather not be.

Love has consequences. Familiar, romantic, friendly, it all shoots you down, burns you, when the time is right. When you're soft and supple, belly up. I hadn't even been home. I took a nap on the couch in my father's room, sleeping when he slept, feeling the drain of the summer sun just as he had. When he woke up, I found my sister gone. I stayed with him through dinner, grabbing a crossword puzzle on the small table next to the couch and working on it.

"What's stumping you, Severin?" my father had asked, pulling my eyes from the little boy in front of me. Tears threatened to fall from my eyes at the sound of my name from his mouth, but I stayed strong. I walked to his bed and we worked on the puzzle together until he fell asleep. I took to the couch in his room and slept a little, too.

When it was time to leave I walked straight from the nursing home to this spot.

My neck aches, and my head is pounding. Sleeping on the couch in my father's room did a number on me. My cross-body purse bounces on my hip as I pick up speed. My hands fumble with the outer flap, reaching for my headphones. I plug them into my phone and pull up my favorite playlist. Classic country songs. They sound different. Clearer, and not as romantic as the records my father played when we did the dishes after Sunday night dinners, but the lyrics are still there, lulling me.

I pick a spot in the grass near the gazebo, check for anthills, squinting my eyes in the night, and take a seat. My bare shoulder hits the cool grass, and my eyes fall closed. I stay like that, familiar songs quieting my aching heart, for a while. A half hour goes by, forty minutes, I'm unsure. I could never do this in New York, or LA. But here, I feel safe, even as my word falls into ruin.

I feel a warm hand on my ankle and whip up, smashing my forehead into the mouth of a man much too close to me. He cusses and I slam both of my palms to my face, ears ringing, eyes spitting salt already.

"I'm sorry! I shouldn't have done that!" Bryan falls back onto his ass from his crouching position.

"What are you doing?" I pull my hands from my face, rip my earphones out.

"I don't know. I saw you lying there, and I wanted to talk to you…"

"So you grabbed my ankle? That's shit people do before they assault someone." My face is painted in anger and I aim it at him.

"I'm sorry, I didn't mean to scare you."

"I know you've lived in Mayberry your whole life, where nothing bad ever happens, but don't ever do that. That's weird AF."

"Did you just say '*AF*'?" He laughs, rubbing his forehead.

"Yes," I reply, unamused.

"That's weird." He smiles, and it causes my lip to turn up, but my heart is still beating out of my chest. I cross my legs at the ankles and eye him. He's so close, smelling of a fresh shower and the faint hint of sawdust. It's like he can't wash it off.

"Why do you want to talk to me? I haven't heard from you in two days. Ready to hear what I have to say about that? I'm sure it'll be loads of fun."

"I imagine that would be a swell time, but no. Let's save it." He crawls over me, and I lean back, giving in without a fight. We swell and touch. His tongue is on my collarbone, pulling my top down. He traces circles there until I am warm and wet, until I am breathless. I push on his chest suddenly, startling him.

"Are you trying to get arrested?"

"Kissing you would get me arrested?"

"Fucking out in the open will get you arrested." I hop up and walk the short distance to the gazebo steps. I take them two at a time. He follows me, walks to me, but I hold up my arm. "Why the radio silence? Regret it? Tell me what you're feeling. Why does it have to be such a goddamn mystery all the time? You're not Jordan Catalano."

He laughs, pulls his hand to his neck. "The dude was super quiet and not that smart. Sounds just like me." He arches an eyebrow at me, a smirk playing on his full lips.

"Shut the fuck up, you watched that?" I lean against a railing, keeping my distance. I do not trust myself.

"Yeah. Au—I didn't pick it."

I don't hate her name. I don't hate her. The right for hatred is not one I can own, but I play the part. "*Oh.* I like a show that Aurora likes? Pardon me. I need to go scrub my brain." I laugh, it sounds strange, for show. I want to pretend I'm not the enemy.

"Dramatic. You're so dramatic."

"Why weren't you in the town square today? Celebrating the queen in all her glory?" Today was the Burlingame Dairy Fest. This town loves their Saturday Festivals. Aurora's family owns the largest dairy farm in the county, just outside of town. The townsfolk gather to celebrate, scurrying in like ants from the various farms surround the city limits. There is music, food, an enthusiastic local band. That's what I remember anyway. I didn't go today. I didn't want to see her, so soon, after screwing her husband. Ben asked me to go, but I refused. I was still avoiding the lunch date he had asked me on. Okay, maybe it wasn't a date he was suggesting, but it still felt weird.

"The town loves Aurora," Bryan says. "So, in turn, they don't like me all that much." He shrugs his shoulders. It's a habit I dislike. So non-committal, so defeatist.

"Doesn't seem fair that only one of you gets custody of the town. And I doubt that's completely true. You're the town realtor, right? That's what you do when you're not fixing up the school?" Ben and I had been texting. I had let him catch me up on a lot of things.

"I'm one of them. I'm not the only option."

"Yeah, but they know you. The people here love you, too."

"I don't know. My mother is sort of dealing with the office stuff now, for me. We are both hoping they'll forget things, the movie and all that." He stares at me, and I stare back, unmoving and unapologetic. "Enough that I won't be missing opportunities. I just gotta lay low for a while. It's all about patience, right?" He shrugs his shoulders, again, and I try not to roll my eyes.

"Is some of my sunny optimism rubbing off on you?" My optimism is for show, half performance, half habit. At least right now it is. There was a time in my life when it was real. But the summer sun cannot make me sunny on the outside.

"I think a lot of you is rubbing off on me. I always thought you would be a good influence on my life. It's part of the reason I was so drawn to you back then. I liked the thought of doing something I was scared of."

I roll my eyes, cross my legs, and go down to the gazebo floor. I stare at his shoes, transfixed. "You say you were scared of me. And I wish I believed it."

"Do you want me to show you?"

"How? If I touch you will you tremble?" I look up into his eyes, a dare. I want him to touch me again. I want to know the night down by the water wasn't a dream, some bullshit I wrote in my head.

"I always do. I just never show my cards." His jaw is set, hands in his pockets. He looks ten years younger, and I feel like a kid again. The most beautiful boy in the world is standing in front of me, and I can have him, if I want. The preacher's son isn't innocent. I know that now, more than ever.

"I don't believe you. Sorry, Jack."

His head is going back and forth, and he begins to pace. "You've been hangin' 'round my brother?"

I blush, feeling caught. "Why do you say that?" I don't deny it, even though it's untrue. We've only texted.

"He always did that as a kid. He gave everyone a million nicknames. So when he was talking about one of his friends, I would get frustrated with him. I never knew who he was talking about."

"I've given him shit about it." But I like it.

"That will just make him want to do it more."

"You don't have to tell me." I watch him lower himself to the floor, too, crawl toward me.

"Do you like him?" he asks.

I lean back, and he crawls over me, his beautiful body is flush against my own. I feel his legs against my own, his arms caging me. "What are you asking me?" He's being jealous, foolish, and I have never seen this side of him. I wrap my legs around him once, and here we are.

"I think you know."

"I just want to hang out tonight. To have fun with you. Let's not ruin it."

"God. Everything has changed, huh? We switched." He untangles, sits down in front of me, close enough to reach out. So he does.

I try not to shiver at the feel of his fingertips, grazing my knees. "How? We fucked, then you ignored me. Sounds right. You take, then run. You leave me with a million wants." I stare at the gazebo ceiling, close my eyes, and focus on his hands.

"I was scared," he says, hushed.

"Maybe that's not so bad though, right? Don't I deserve it? To be the one in control?" I let him push my knees apart.

"To be chased?" His hands are insistent, so I let go. I let him kiss the inside of my thighs, where I'm nothing but sweat and frustration. "Yes. Yes, you do deserve it. But I hope it isn't a game."

"Everything is a game," I say, letting go.

WHATEVER HAPPENS

PAST

HIS CLOTHES WERE CHANGED. DENIM JEANS, UNTIED tennis shoes, an unbuttoned flannel. I loved him that way. I approached hesitantly. His head was buried in his hands and no one sat near him. The wide berth they gave Bryan should have been a warning, but this vulnerability drew me closer. I felt eyes on me. My skin had been buzzing all night long. They were watching us closely. Trying to figure the puzzle out. I was doing the same.

"Go over there," Christina had urged, the odd man out. Britt and Akia argued I should leave him alone. That everyone was watching us and I didn't need a target on my back. I already had one, as far as I was concerned. It didn't matter.

"This is a shit show," Britt mumbled.

"An epic one," Akia echoed.

"So what?" Christina took my hand.

I ran my other sweaty palm over the silk of my dress. My curls were falling. The pictures were done, and I was coming undone. Any time

I heard someone laugh I wondered if it was at my expense. Then I wondered why I cared. "He looks sad." I hated the way my voice sounded, but I couldn't change who I was.

"He does," Christina said, squeezing my hand. "Go talk to him. No one is talking to him."

"Because *they* are smart," Britt scoffed.

"I want you to know, Sev, I think you're brave," Christina said, pulling my eye to her.

"No."

"Yes. You went up to him and you asked him to be your escort. You didn't chicken out like you said you wanted to a million times. You just did the damn thing. And tonight has been weird and crazy and I know it sucks in a lot of ways. But you did the thing you were scared of. Something I could never do. So now you need to do the other thing you are scared to do."

"No."

"Yes."

I groaned, feeling Britt and Akia's eyes on us. I didn't look at them. Instead, I looked at Bryan again. His sad air and his pale skin. I cleared my throat and stood, running my hand over the wrinkles in my dress.

I walked across the gym without a word to my friends and sat next to him. I wrung my hands together and turned back, looking into Christina's eyes. She motioned for me to speak, but I couldn't. I shook my head back and forth, widened my eyes. Next to me, Bryan moved, pulled his hands through his hair, along his neck. Did he know the effect these simple movements had on people? The way our eyes followed his hands, his slow and sure wanderings?

"How are you?" I echoed his words from the river.

"Not good." He didn't need to say more. I'd heard the whispers. A romance I was unsure of, now confirmed. Something was going on between him and Aurora. It should have deterred me, but here I was. My lips still felt his. My body was lingering in the past.

"I'm sorry." It wasn't a lie. I could feel his grief, his body was so close, I wanted to touch him. To absorb his pain. "Do you want to dance?" It was absurd. The gossip was thick in the room, but I wanted to be selfish. I wanted to be closer to him. To touch him while I could. I knew, without a doubt, that when this night was over, we would go back to our normal. He would walk by me in the halls, and we wouldn't speak. Maybe the looks would stop after this, with the eyes of the student body trained on us more than ever.

"Okay." He stood up, surprising me. He turned when he reached the gym floor, his hand reaching for me.

If I never saw him again after graduation, this is what I would remember. His slender fingers, his pale wrist. I wanted to know what love was, so I took that hand.

We walked out to the dance floor. The hair at the back of my neck stood on end. Eyes and whispers echoed around me. It all quieted when his hands found my waist, when my own wanting fingers touched his neck.

"I want you to know that I'm sorry." The words came out before I could stop them. I was sorry. I truly was. My own desires were nothing compared to the want for his happiness. For this melancholy air to leave his presence.

"For what?" His mouth was near my ear, his chin was up.

"For ruining whatever was going on with you and Aurora."

"Severin, you didn't kiss me. I kissed you. Whatever happens, this is my doing." His voice was monotone, autopilot assurance. These were the things that kept me tethered to him. The things that made me wonder how Christina could be so infatuated with someone like Rodney. I liked Bryan because behind all of it—his popularity and his disarming smile—was a kindness.

"Whatever happens," I repeated.

"Yes. Whatever happens between her and I."

"You and Aurora. Yes. Do you love her?" It would be a silly question if it weren't for the knowledge we both had. Their shared past. Their titles. Their likeness. Their beauty.

His hands tensed on my hips. "I'm eighteen." It wasn't an answer. We both knew that.

"So am I. I think we can be in love at this age. It's not impossible. Some people find their soulmates in high school. It's crazy and kind of cute," I rambled on, feeling him shaking his head. A polite nodding. "Like my parents. And Britt's parents, too. My sister didn't meet her girlfriend here. Finding her soulmate in Burlingame High was out of the question, but stranger things have happened." I needed to stop talking about random shit. The song was going to end soon, and I would find myself at home dissecting this moment and wondering why I spoke about who met in high school and the fact that my sister was gay. *God. Why was I like this?*

"Yeah. Maybe it's possible for some." I felt his grip on me lessen a little, and I thought I felt him shiver. I'd scared him, and maybe he was wondering how far this crush went. I caught the eyes of my friends around his shoulder. They were watching our every move. Or, Britt and Akia were. I saw Christina eyeing Rodney. He was sitting a few seats down on the bleachers from her, being loud and intolerable.

I wondered where Aurora had run off to. She left after the crowning ceremony.

They made sense in a way Bryan and I never would. We could try as hard as we wanted to rewrite the rules of high school, but the crowns we were taking weren't changing things in the end.

It felt good. It was fun when it wasn't terrifying. And everyone but the beautiful and chosen ones applauded us. We were a new kind of royalty. The kind you could relate to. The kind who didn't wear name brands and drive flashy cars and jacked up trucks to school. Hell, I still walked to school or rode the bus. My father wasn't budging on a vehicle at all. He worried way too much.

My friends and I, we weren't getting dates with the beautiful boys. We were basically the same people. If I weren't dancing with Bryan, I would be sitting on the bleachers with them, cracking jokes and eyeing him from afar. I suddenly wanted to be with them, away from Bryan and all we could never be. The song wasn't over, but I pulled away. I looked up into Bryan's eyes, and I felt red, raw.

"Thank you for agreeing to be my escort. Thank you for walking me in and being so nice. Thank you for dancing with me, when that was the last thing you should do. It was selfish of me to ask."

"It's fine." His eyes reached mine, then flittered away. "I mean, you're welcome." His face was pained and I hated my part in it.

"Have a nice night." I walked away, back to my friends. Back to where I belonged. I barely felt his hand graze mine as I left him. And when I looked across the gym, I saw his younger brother watching me.

LOST TIME

I DON'T COME BY WHEN BRYAN HAS HIS DAUGHTER. IT'S an unspoken rule. I see her on the lawn of the school. I see her jumping rope on the sidewalk. I watch from the window as Bryan races her back and forth. Every day, for a week they do this. I wonder if she is interested in the track team. Her mother was.

I write down the things they do. It's a habit, a people watching habit. I always carry a moleskin notebook in my back pocket when I leave the house. I can only write believable characters in my work by absorbing others. This is the relationship I am most familiar with, watching them takes me back. A father and a daughter. A smiling girl. His daughter has light hair. Like him. Like her mother's. Sometimes I see Bryan glance at my house. I wonder what he wonders. I debate taking Beau for a walk. Casually running into them across the street. But I cannot insert myself into this part of his life. I cannot latch on.

Today I push boundaries. I take my coffee onto the front porch. I drink it slowly, reading the newspaper. It's what my father did, though never in the mornings, but I need to feel close to him. At night, I will bring him the paper so he can have his routine. So I can be a part of it.

Across the street Bryan and his daughter are loud. They have a hose, and they laugh as they wash his truck. His truck that never moves. It's so odd.

My sister walks outside, catching me. "I wasn't sure where you were. I smelled the coffee. God, I needed it. I was up way too late last night going through photos. Dad took so many. I miss those days. Everyone has their pictures on their phones now. I'm glad I went to school before cell phones and all of that."

"Yeah. You're a fossil now, aren't you?" I laugh to myself.

"Watch it. You're no spring chicken." She takes a seat next to me.

"Thirty is the new twenty. Didn't you know?"

"Ah, to be thirty again."

"The middle ages must have been nice. Cozy."

"Your *'you're old'* jokes are running out of steam. They're kind of lame these days."

I shrug. "You're right."

"You're obsessing." She stares ahead, looking where I won't look.

"Yes."

"What is it about him, anyway? I've never actually seen him in person. He looks…yeah, I guess I can see the appeal. Nice arms. He's tall."

"If you were into boys, would you be into him?"

"No. I've heard too many of your stories. He sounds wishy-washy and I don't have time for that shit. Find someone who is sure of you and you're golden."

"I'm glad you have that. I miss living with you guys."

"We miss having you. It's a little boring without your drama. I called Amber last night and told her the latest on you."

I laugh at her. "I didn't have drama. I had...exciting stories. And did she have my back this time? She always did."

"That's the thing," she says, ignoring my question. "You know those people who say they hate drama? Those are the people who have the most drama in their lives. And, sister, you have a shit ton. And you bring it on yourself, really. I think you need it."

"Ouch." I fold the newspaper, set it on the table between our chairs.

"No one knows you like I do, Sev. You can move away and you can hide in your words and you can create a shit storm of epic proportions. But I will always know who you are and I will point out what needs to be pointed out."

"Okay. You're right. And this is why I fucking love you, honestly."

"You ever have that lunch with the brother?" I showed her Ben's Facebook profile. We talked about my past with him. The way he saved me from a shit night and a lone walk into a gym of staring eyes. Did I ever thank him properly? Maybe that was long overdue.

"No," I reply, watching Bryan. "Maybe I will today." I reach for my phone, search for Ben's number. It's nine a.m. and I don't feel hungry. I often drink coffee for breakfast when I'm feeling self-destructive. When I'm lost in the mess of my life. And things are getting messier and messier now.

"That's a good idea. I want to have lunch with Dad alone today."

"You ditching me?"

"No. I just, sometimes I get so caught up in worrying about you, I can't focus on him fully."

"I'm a big girl, Sash. You don't have to worry about me." But I know she is right. I've seen her do this for me too many times.

"That's never going to happen. I just, I want a lunch alone with Dad."

"It's no big deal. I was just messing with you. I'll see if Ben is free. Maybe then I can go into town without worrying about an ambush."

"From?"

"Aurora. I am so fucking paranoid now."

"Well..." She trails off, eyeing the water fight across the street. "She has her mother's hair."

"Yep."

"Yep."

————

Later, at the urging of my sister, I find myself sitting at a tiny white wrought iron table outside of Betty's Bakery. I bring Beau, and Ben, my lunch date, goes inside to order our sub sandwiches. When he returns he startles me with a revelation as I bite into my sandwich.

"You know, I always had a thing for you. And you always had a thing for my brother. But I knew it wouldn't work out between you two." He pulls a piece of pepperoni from his sandwich and throws it to Beau.

"Maybe it's working out now." I'm trying to convince myself, more than him. I don't know what is going on in my life, but I want to get lost in the tangling. The drama, as my sister called it, distracts me from the sadness sitting around our house.

"Oh, yeah? Because you're fucking?" He grins, sauce on his face.

"Don't be so crass." I don't get riled up at his words, a reaction I'm sure he was trying to pull. He doesn't know who he is messing with. And it's too new to name it, but he may not be wrong. I motion for him to wipe his mouth.

"Did I offend your delicate self?" He grabs a napkin and cleans himself up.

"No," I say, lifting the bread off my sandwich, looking for the olives I told him I didn't want.

"No. Okay, you just don't want me to say it that way. It's the truth, though. Listen, I have no doubt he likes you. He always has. And this has been a long time coming...but it's just fucking. You've always wanted each other. But this is a fling. It can't be anything more, Sevvy, you know that."

I laugh. "This is a wonderful way to start out our new friendship, asshole." I don't mind his forwardness. It reminds me of the one other person here I wish I could be close to. Britt always told me how it was, told me the things I wanted to hide from. "Okay. So who should I be with? You? Since you've had a crush on me since high school?"

"Okay, yes, I did have a thing for you back then, but I didn't like, pine for you after you graduated or I graduated. It's school. It doesn't matter. And I don't have a thing for you now."

"So if I wanted to fuck, you wouldn't be into it?" I look around to see if the other outside table is occupied. It isn't.

"Well, I'm not stupid, Sevvy." He looks at me hard, his eyes slowly taking me in, and look away.

"You were so wild back then. And sweet, to me anyway." I roll my eyes, my cheeks a little red. *Why is he having this effect on me?*

"I was sixteen. And I'm sweet now, too. I get it, you don't like the things I'm saying. Doesn't make them any less true."

"Well, thank you for your words of wisdom." I grab my phone and text Sasha, asking how her lunch with Dad is going. Telling her it was a mistake to have lunch with Ben. I like that we can say whatever we want to each other, that it feels like we have known each other our whole lives, and we have known of each other, but that's not the same thing. When I'm done texting I stand, gathering my paper plate and utensils.

"You're leaving?"

"Yeah." I wasn't planning to, but I lie anyway. "Too much truth serum I guess. I don't feel much like hanging out anymore." I reach for my purse, but he shoots off two words. They halt me. Because I want him to halt me, to say anything.

"Wanna dance?" He motions across the street, to the center of town.

"What?" I can't even look at the gazebo the same way now. There is an elderly group taking dancing lessons on the grass of the square. Are they waltzing?

"For old times' sake. Like prom."

"No." I want to. I want the connection. Something less angry and heated.

"Why? Afraid my brother will find out?"

"Stop being an ass."

"I know you are. You don't want to disrupt this image of you waiting for him. It's all he's ever known, and it's all you've ever known how to be."

"I didn't think about your brother when I moved away. Is this the kind of friendship you were looking to have with me? Because it isn't fun at all." I decide to leave in earnest. I throw my trash into the outside bin next to our table, start untying Beau's leash from our table.

"Really? You didn't think about him when you wrote a play about him? When you adapted it into a screenplay? You didn't think about it when you saw the movie?"

He's laughing, and I find it hard to be mad at him. He's so good at what he does. At setting himself apart from his brother who is quiet and melancholy and simmering passion. I finally go, to feel the passion. "Okay. For real. I'm leaving now. I'm not mad, asshole. But, I need to go hang out at home, so I'm there when my sister gets back from having lunch with my father."

"Okay. For real, how is he?"

"He's...okay." I don't know what to say. Progress reports are something I only share with my aunt, with Sasha. Bryan has acknowledged my father's situation, but has he asked me how he is? I rack my brain, searching for an answer that I can stomach.

Ben stands, shoving the last of his sandwich in his mouth. A couple walks by, and he says hello to them, starts a conversation. They are familiar with each other, but I cannot place them. I stay rooted in place. Waiting for him to be done so I can give him a proper goodbye.

He waves to the couple and turns to me, bends at the knees, and starts petting the hair around Beau's ears, resuming his train of thought. *God, he fascinates me.* "So we make love a tragedy. We make it a walking nightmare. Or, at least, some of us do. Is it only the poets? The romantics? People like you?"

"How did you know I'm a poet? I haven't written a poem in years." I try not to think of the drivel that poured out of me back then.

"It's the way you talk. You can't hide it. You can't hide it from someone like me anyway." He stands, smiling at my dog.

"I imagine hiding from someone like you is impossible," I say, drawing his eyes upward. "You see things. And it's because your eyes aren't pointed inward. You're not all wrapped up in your inner turmoil. It's refreshing. I want to be like that. Less dramatic. Less caught up in this storm." I think of my sister and the way she points everything out. She would like Ben.

"See, poetry." He smiles. "If you look at the people who hurt you, and the ways they hurt you, that will teach you a lot. Don't mimic those habits. The ones they use to wound you."

"I don't want to do the things he does." My lunch tasted stale, the way it often does when I'm stressed out. When I'm taking on too much and making more jokes than usual. Making more distractions.

"Then don't," he says.

"Thanks for lunch. I'm sorry I was dramatic for a bit there."

"I like that about you." He laughs, so musical.

"Okay, I'll see you later." I get a few steps, nearly making it to the crosswalk, then hear Ben's voice again.

"Tell my brother I said hi when you see him later."

I don't turn around.

————

The gym looks the same, different. It looks sad, and I feel that inside me. The sound of the basketball bouncing on the court ripples through me later that night when I sneak over to the school.

Bryan's head is down, the hair falling over his forehead. There is a can of beer on the edge of the court.

"Something I do is come here and I think about that night. I still don't know what I should have done. If I had never kissed you, I never would have known what it was like to kiss you. But if I hadn't kissed you, I wouldn't have hurt her. Or you. I've never been that good at choosing in life. I obsess and pick over my options. I got that from my father's presence. I didn't think about it that night, the way he made me go over my options and the path I could take with every decision. I just knew I wanted to kiss you and I did it. I didn't care about the consequences. I'm still paying for that night. I saw it today, with my daughter."

She's upstairs, staying with her father. The reason for my late-night visit, the reason I had to sneak in quietly.

"I'm supposed to be sorry, right?" I whisper, as if she can hear me and the stories, above us.

"You didn't do anything wrong. I just look at you, and I want to be more. When I look at her, I just want to be me. Simple as that. I want to be who she thinks I am. You make me want to reach. Maybe that's why I'm still here. I didn't choose you, so I stayed put. I stayed still and failed."

"Failed at what?" I sit down on the court, look up at him.

"Life. I've done nothing." He spreads his arms wide, shakes his head.

"I wish you wouldn't beat yourself up. Were you like this back then? I feel like I only got a piece of you. The confident, quiet guy. The one who touched me and made me shiver."

"I made you nervous." There is a small smile playing his lips. I like knowing I put it there.

"Yes." I would turn red, run over my words. I would lose my breath and forget my name. He did that to me. He was poetry and perfection. I wanted to devour him.

"You make me nervous. You did then, you do now. Maybe I didn't show it. But it's true. You want more, Severin. You don't sit idle."

He throws the basketball in the air, catches it, turns to me. How beautiful he is. Long and lithe. I want to crawl inside of him. To find the pieces he deems unworthy.

"I'm glad you weren't the one."

"What do you mean?" His jaw is set, preparing for the hurt.

"The one I lost my virginity to."

He laughs, soft and crinkled around the eyes. "I'm glad I wasn't either. I'm sure I was shit in bed back then."

"And now?" I stand, walk to him.

"I don't know. Care to tell me?" He drops the ball, gathers me. He tastes like mint and beer. Forgiveness and the hint of a grudge I won't let go of.

It was that first thrust that did me in, down by the water. Like I had been holding my breath, for years, waiting for him. Waiting for this moment. A validation. A reminder of all I held onto. Maybe this was why I never fell in love, not entirely. My two-year relationship, the only one to my name, was forgotten. I never felt this with my ex. I never felt this release.

"Fuck." Bryan's breath is on my neck. I push my shoulder blades into the gym floor, look up at him. He moves slowly, his forearms caging me. I grip them, their heat is addicting. I run my fingers over the veins there, it nearly unravels me.

"Why?" It's the only word I get out; it stutters past my lips as I breathe.

"Why what?" He pulls back, resting his forehead on mine.

"Why did we wait so long for this? I love this." I'm embarrassed by the words tumbling out. There is no guard. There should be. I should rein it in, but a large part of me doesn't want to. If these are the only times, it will be enough. In the heat of this, I try to convince myself this is my truth. *No one should ever be put in the shadows.* I close my eyes to keep out the shadows of the gym.

Bryan laughs, slows, pulls away. "I've wanted to do this for a while." It's not the most romantic thing a girl has ever heard, but I don't mind. I would be okay with the silence, the heavy sound of our breathing, our bodies connecting, disconnecting.

We are on a dirty floor, just feet from the place he first kissed me. It's wrong on so many levels, and that fuels me. My hair on my face, my bra pushed up, Bryan's jeans pushed down. I imagine myself remembering this years later. Regret may paint it in hues I cannot see now. It may not.

I pull Bryan's neck, bite his lip. "Let's make up for lost time."

I'M SORRY I KISSED YOU

PAST

TWO MONDAYS AFTER HOMECOMING, I SAW THEM. AURORA and Bryan. Hands intertwined, lips pressed together before class. My heart broke. I broke. I was so good at keeping it all in, though.

The proof was in the way my eyes never swayed. The way I avoided Bryan's face in class. The way I stared at my feet when he passed me in the hall.

I could feel his eyes on me. I could feel a reaching out. He wanted me to look up. He wanted something from me, but I wouldn't give in. I confessed my assumptions to my friends at lunch one day, when the bubbling over felt too loud.

"He keeps staring at me, right? I can feel it. Maybe I'm making it up." I gripped my tray with my left hand, stirred my runny mashed potatoes aggressively with my right.

"He keeps looking at you. Like, these little bullshit glances. When his face isn't attached to Aurora's." Britt sounded bitter, carrying my rage, my heartbroken humming.

"Okay, so at least we know I'm not insane."

"Debatable." Christina nudged me, trying to cheer me up.

I'd been a downer since homecoming. I didn't want to talk on the phone, and I didn't talk in the halls. I carried my broken heart around, heavy on my shoulders. I wrote poetry until late at night. My father would rap his knuckles on my door, ordering me to turn my lamp off.

The bags under my eyes were dark, unbecoming. I needed to snap out of it. This was a silly high school love. I didn't get the boy. It happens all the time, and it's not a tragedy. I reminded myself of these things every day.

"This isn't a tragedy," I mumbled, pulling my eyes from my mess of food.

"No. It's not. He's a stupid fucking boy. And he picked the wrong girl," Christina said confidently.

I shook my head. "It was never a choice. Remember, he didn't like me. He was just being polite."

"I don't believe that. You don't jam your tongue down someone's throat to be polite." Britt propped her head on her hand, glanced Bryan's way. "He acted so freaking weird around you. And when he picked you up that night, just to make sure you knew he wasn't going to be a caveman and slap your ass. Then the dancing at homecoming!"

I held my hands up, halting her. "We can't go down this road again. Trust me, I do this in my head every damn day. I'm so tired of over-analyzing it all."

"Chapter closed?" Christina grabbed her boxed milk and held it to the center of the table. We all grabbed ours, toasted to the decision. A chapter closed.

———

He found me later, during my free period. I was in my usual spot, behind the red curtain. I didn't know it was him coming in the auditorium. I heard the door open and close, but it didn't register to me. Students came in and out all the time.

I noticed his shoes first. His unlaced Nikes. One of his touchstones. One of the things I would always associate with him. They were right in front of me, so I stared at them for a moment. Refusing to look up. Bryan cleared his throat, moved his weight from his right foot to his left. I heard him say *hi*, so I reluctantly looked up, clutching my notebook to my chest. "What brings you here?"

"I wanted to see how you are." He said it simply, like it was something he did all the time. As if we were friends in some other life. As if it was simmering over into this one. The one where we couldn't talk in the halls, couldn't be friends in any way.

"I'm fine." We both knew I wasn't, but I needed to say it. I hated looking up at him, and I could tell it made him uncomfortable, too. I didn't break eye contact as he lowered himself down onto the stage floor. "I suppose it's okay for you to be with me here then. You know, since no one can see you." I was bitter. Bitter over his new relationship.

"We both know no one would like it."

"Do you know I don't care anymore?" I pulled my legs in, crossed them at the ankles. My notebook was shoved behind my back, distanced. The words there would be safe. But I was not, sitting here in front of him.

"About me?" He pointed at himself as if I wouldn't know what the hell he was talking about.

"I mean, all of it. But why would you ask me if I don't care about you? I don't think you have a right to know that answer anymore. You have a girlfriend. The feelings of any other girl are a non-issue now. Those feelings are officially off limits for you to know." I pointed at him, angry and showing it. I didn't care anymore.

"Yeah, I get it. You're repeating yourself."

"Just want to make sure you know."

"How am I an ass for coming to see how you are?"

"Because it's so fucking arrogant. You're just walking around thinking you shattered me or something." My voice was rising. I wondered if Kenny, a saxophone player in the school band, was in the room. He liked to come practice here on his own. I hadn't seen him come in today.

"I'm not trying to be arrogant, or an ass. I'm just trying to be nice."

"Well, trying to be nice and just *being* nice, are two different things. You think just because you're the preacher's son and you don't say much means you're good. But maybe it just means you were raised to be good, and you hide the bad. Don't they say preachers' kids are actually the worst? Maybe that's true." I stood up. I couldn't be near him. I couldn't handle his heavy presence, the way my body reacted to him. The pouty lips and the sad eyes. The ivory skin and the way he smelled. Like clean clothes and spice.

"I'm sorry I kissed you," he said, standing, too.

His voice was low, and he didn't sound like he meant it. It sounded like he regretted the way it made me feel. But I couldn't be sure. Because I always defended him in the end. It was a weakness of mine.

————

Later that night, Britt dropped me off after having dinner at her house. I found a bouquet of roses on my doorstep—yellow. I grabbed them and walked to my bedroom window. I placed them on the windowsill so I could grab them when I got inside. I didn't want to explain their presence to my father. I didn't want to give him more proof of my broken heart. That someone liked leaving roses, but wouldn't pull me from the shadows.

We were having a bowl of ice cream before bed when I decided to ask him about my mother. It had been a while since I brought up the past, went digging.

"So, Mom had a thing for you when she had another boyfriend, right? That's what you said?"

My father ran the tip of his spoon over the edge of the bowl, his eyes were aimed at the living room. The news was playing softly in the background. He blinked twice, and I could see the wrinkles on his face more prominently. His age was more apparent. It made me sad. I wondered what he would do in our little house when I left, so soon.

"She had a crush on me. For a while. Yes."

"And you didn't have a crush on her? You were too wrapped up with the girlfriend she noticed you with?"

"Yes. I only had eyes for the girl I was with. And your mother, she was shy, and she painted. I ran track and hung out with some assholes. I was an idiot. When she told me she'd had a crush on me for a while, it was a surprise."

"How long did she have a crush on you before you felt the same?"

"Too long. Eventually, I broke up with my girlfriend and your mother got tired of her boyfriend. Sometimes stupid boys don't know what's best for them. That boy was stupid, and I was also stupid at times. Promise me you won't fall for a stupid boy."

I regretted asking. I was rewarded with more fuel for my fading fire. And it was too late for me. I had already fallen for a stupid boy. *Chapter closed.*

FAKE IT 'TIL YOU MAKE IT

"CHAPTER CLOSED." MY SISTER LET THE BOOK IN HER hand close.

She's being clinical. This is her version of being strong. For my benefit, no doubt. But it isn't working.

She places the book in the box at her feet, and I feel a shiver ripple through me. I'm standing in the kitchen, with a cup of coffee in my hands. The steam warms my face, my nostrils flare. I can only have a few sips. Then it will go down the drain. I don't need the jitters that accompany this vice. I don't need my mind wandering.

"Maybe you can live here?" I look at my aunt, standing in the hall with a hamper full of laundry sitting on her hip. Her eyes pull from Sasha, the same look of wonder there. One of wondering why she is being so stoic. She shakes her head, finds my eyes.

"No, Sev. This isn't my town, and I'm just not up for finding my place in a new community again." She turns and walks back down the hall to the laundry room. The silence envelopes me and my sister. I feel raw, my skin is pink and pulsing from my early morning shower. Pulsing from the way Bryan is pulling me.

"You got in late last night." It's a fact. There's no question there.

"Yeah." I pull my old chair out, take a seat. "I was talking to Ben Winthrop."

I spend my nights with Ben when Bryan is busy with his daughter. Last night we drove two towns over to the drive-in movie theater. We ate popcorn and didn't plug our headphones in; instead, we narrated the movie with our own stories. I laughed until I nearly pissed myself. Our friendship distracted me from everything. The sex with Bryan should have been a distraction from the heavy in my life, but it just added to my turmoil. My aching stomach and tense neck.

"Have fun?" Her little mask drops and I hear it.

"Yes." I pause. "Are you okay?"

"No. I hate being here." She places another item in the box. "And that makes me feel guilty. I miss my love, and my little girl, and I miss Dad but it's like he isn't even here. Just evidence of his existence."

"I know what you mean. At night I replay our phone calls. I remember his handwritten letters. I brought them with me. They're in my trunk. I want to put them in the hatbox, with Mom's letters."

"That's a good idea." She keeps placing books in the box at her feet. Books we will donate, books maybe I will take home. "I wonder if Mom would have been a worrier. All through our teenage years and when we bought our first homes. Suffered the latest heartache. Heard our children laugh for the first time."

Sasha has been through the milestones a mother would worry over. More than me. "I think she would have been a worrier, but also would have encouraged us to take risks. The same way Dad did. I think he always had her in mind when he was guiding us."

"I worry for you." She places the large dictionary in the box.

"Why?"

"It'll always be there, Sev. It's what mothers do."

I close my eyes over the steam of my coffee, quickly ghosting away. "I don't worry for me. I'm not a little girl anymore. And you taught me to be strong. So did Dad."

"Two boys? You're not worried for yourself?" She smiles, and I laugh, throaty and squinty-eyed.

"It's not how it looks. One is a friend."

"And one is the boy you've loved for over ten years. Nothing to worry about, eh?"

"Yeah. Nothing to worry about." I take one last warm sip of my coffee.

————

"Tell me about the things you're addicted to," I say to Ben as I sink one of my balls into a corner pocket. The jukebox at Falcon's Nest plays a One Republic song in the back room where two pool tables sit. We're the only ones here at two p.m.

"Running away from relationships. Avoiding my family. Folk music. New dark denim. Converse. Live music. Tiny little cigars. Blondes. Riding my bike with no hands on the wheel."

"Those are some nice things." I straighten, eyeing the table, looking for my next target.

"Those are some nice things, yes. Maybe we both stayed away from the bad shit for the same reasons. You had a ghost talking to you, and I had my father in the next room. Telling my mother she wasn't worth a damn and would never amount to anything if she left him. That no one would support the woman who left the town preacher broken-hearted."

"Shame is a powerful motivator." I listen when Ben tells me the truth about his pastor father and his mother. A truth I was never aware of. When I press Bryan for information, I get little in return. The only time I find him pliable is right after sex, which seems unfair.

"Yes. And another powerful drug. I wish he had just stuck to alcohol. Let it destroy him and only him." When Ben speaks of his father he is very matter of fact, almost clinical, but I can still hear it. The little hints of regret. Resentment. Rage.

"Sometimes when I'm near you, or your brother, I can feel your feelings for him rolling off you like waves." I miss my next shot, my mind elsewhere, thinking of fading memories. Or the way the mind can wither.

"Are they the same?"

"No. Yours is anger. Bryan's is regret, sadness."

"He never could be as pissed as me."

"I think it was hard on him. Taking care of you and your mom and himself." I've glued together a story. Pieced their scraps into something readable. I need stories, true or fiction, it doesn't matter, to distract from my own.

"I'm grateful. Don't get me wrong." He misses his shot. He isn't as good at pool as I am. My friends and I hung out here all the time. He was too cool for this place.

"Then what is it? Why do you hate him so much?" I've asked Bryan the same, and I'm rewarded with anger. He closes down. The sex becomes more heated. He is easy to manipulate, and I imagine that's how he saw me back then. He's right, perhaps. We have switched.

"I don't hate him. I never have. You don't get it. You have a sister, right?"

"Yes." I walk to our booth, grab a fry, and bite into it. It's gone cold.

"Do you guys ever fight?"

"Not like you two do. If she takes my curling iron, I get a little snippy, maybe. But she was like a mother to me. She helped raise me, and she's a bit older than me."

"Maybe it's a guy thing."

"Don't be typical. Don't be a cliché."

"I'm sorry I'm boring you. Some people like clichés. They're comforting." He laughs, not rising the way Bryan would at the word.

"You're not boring, but you're... I don't know..." I think of his brother and the cycles we repeat. "I need you to surprise me. I'm addicted to surprises." I watch him walk to me, take his seat. He leans forward and rewards me with his wide smile.

"Two boring addicts walk into a bar..."

I cut him off. "Don't call us that. We don't suffer. So many suffer. We are fucking lucky, you hear me?"

"I do. And I know it."

"Let's get out of here." My voice sounds strange. Like I'm suggesting something. And maybe I am. I'm tired of the games Bryan and I play. With Ben, it's easy. It's fun. It isn't torturous, and I don't want to cry when I leave him, I don't want to shower off shame, and I don't want to pull my brain from my skull, smash it on the curb.

"Where to, Sevvy?"

"Did you do all the things popular kids did in school? I wish I could say I knew what you were like back then. But it's just a glimmer. You were younger, and I was walking around with my head in the clouds or halfway up your brother's ass."

"It's nice to see things have changed." Ben grabs his wallet and fishes out a twenty, dropping it on the table next to our check.

"Oh, shut up. I have the upper hand now, maybe." I wink at him.

"Denial looks good on you." He musses my hair, and I wish then that I had more guy friends. I've never really had one.

"Okay, maybe I don't. But seriously. Tell me." I walk out of the Falcon's Nest, and it feels good to be seen with a Winthrop boy. To be out of hiding.

"Like what kinds of things?"

"Parties, sex, alcohol, cruising." He raises his hand to his mouth like I'm being scandalous, so I punch him in the arm.

"That, yeah, I did those things. Why?"

"I don't know. I guess I wanted you to show me one of those things, but now that I've listed them all out, I realize I've done those things. Maybe it was later in life, but I see now that I wasn't missing it then. You know, I can't even fathom teenagers having sex. It horrifies me.

Because I know I wasn't ready back then. Who did you lose it to?" I reach the passenger door of Ben's Jeep and open it, staring through to the other side. Ben hops in and looks over at me. I'm wagging my eyes like an idiot.

"Farrah Gustaf. Get in."

"Oh, she was cute!" I slam the door and reach for my seat belt.

He raises an eyebrow. "Very. And experienced. Willing to teach my dumb ass a thing or two. Want me to show you what she taught me?"

"Shut up. C'mon. Let's go. Let's get out of here." I grab his keys from his hand and push them into the ignition.

———

We end up down by the creek. I shiver, and it's not just the water that makes me reach for the jacket I have in his back seat.

Ben skips rocks and seems oblivious to my body tremors.

The first time I was here, I was a shy virgin. And I was with his brother. The second time I was here, I was having sex against a tree. And I was with his brother.

I'm playing with fire. I've always known it, but it hits me full force.

I like them both, and I have been trying to deny it. They say the heart wants what it wants, but I'm not sure what she is saying right now. It's more like my fucking loins. I want them both, and the fact that they are brothers makes me seriously wonder what the fuck is wrong with me. Is this what kinky is? No. I've never considered myself that word. Maybe I am just a little…selfish.

They clearly have their issues, and I'm becoming one of them. Or maybe that's my arrogance talking. My newfound arrogance that Bryan says I have acquired.

He is an ass. It's not arrogance. He just can't handle the fact that I grew a backbone. That being away from this small town and the cliques and cheerleaders made me realize that none of that shit matters.

I'm pulled from my thoughts when my situation gets a little shittier. I see Ben taking his shirt off by the end of the bridge.

"What the fuuuuuck are you doing, bro?"

"I'm not your bro." He takes his shoe off, hopping on the other.

"As long as you call me whatever the hell you want, I'm doing the same, Benjamin."

"Hey, I like that. It's sexy. Makes me sound smart." The other shoe is gone.

I roll my eyes, remembering he truly had everything in high school. "You *are* smart."

"Marry me." His pants come off. *Good god.*

"I'll marry you if you stop taking your clothes off."

"Okay, I know you've never been married, but that's the opposite of how it works."

"Seriously though," my face heats as I watch him. "What are you doing?"

"I'm unburdening myself. One sock at a time." He throws a sock in my direction, and I dodge it, barely.

"What are you unburdening yourself of?" I hate to admit it, but Ben excites me—everything he says, everything he does, the way he moves.

"Clothes. Expectations. Hereditary traits. Dreams. Lies. False hope."

"Do you feel lighter yet?" I walk in his direction.

"Yes. Just speaking it out loud. You should try."

"To unburden myself or to take my clothes off in front of you?"

H shrugs his shoulder, eyeing me. "Whatever makes you feel better."

"You should have taken me here after prom. I would have cried less." I remember the night, his attempts to make me smile. The burn of alcohol down my throat. He succeeded then. He succeeds every time I see him now.

"It was the rainy season."

"Would have been a great reason to take that dress off." I reach for the hem of my shirt, pretend I'm going to take it off.

"Don't do that." Ben's face is serious.

"Do what?" I drop my shirt.

"Rewrite the past in your mind, in casual conversation. Don't pretend it was different. The sooner you see things for how they are, the better."

"And how are they? How are things?"

"I think you know. But the lie is sweeter." He blows me a kiss.

"What's the lie?" I'm no longer distracted by Ben's body, his mouth. I'm focused on his words.

"He likes you."

"You don't think he does?" I cross my arms, widen my stance.

"He likes parts of you. He likes the parts of you he wishes he had in himself. Traits he thinks will wash all over him, and he thinks he can absorb you."

"Maybe that's okay?" I want to convince myself, but when he says it like that, I know the truth.

"If you want to be his personal good mojo scrub, okay. Go for it."

"Maybe I do. It's just for the summer, right?"

"It doesn't take long to scar someone. And it'll just be one scar right over another one. At least let someone new take a crack at it."

"I can't tell if you are hitting on me, if you just want what he has, or if this is just the way you talk. I don't even know you, if you think about it. I didn't know you then, and I don't know you now."

"You know me now. Don't worry about little sixteen-year-old Ben."

"Okay."

"And don't worry about teenage Bryan and teenage Severin. Stop this obsessing."

"Okay."

"It creeps me out when you agree with me."

"Okay." I bite my lip.

"Stop it."

I flirt despite the warning in my head. "Yes, sir."

"Okay, that just turns me on."

"Stop! I don't want to see it!" I let go of my angry stance, raise my palms, so they are blinding my line of sight to his dick, covered in nothing but tight boxer briefs.

"Okay, okay. Let's just relax and quit talking."

"No matter what you say it just sounds like you're hitting on me now."

"Get in the water. It'll feel good to get wet."

"I hate you." I strip.

————

The water feels good. My skin is still a little sunburnt, and it soothes when nothing feels soothing these days.

Ben spins in the water, his mouth just under the surface.

"Do you feel unburdened?" His cocksure grin makes me warm again. I like his friendship. I expected to come home to a friend, but I was wrong. I love my sister, but I don't want to burden her with any of my worries or sadness. She carries too much on her shoulders.

I shrug. "I feel...warm."

"Warm is good, right?"

"I don't know. I feel like I've been living in fucking hell here. Did you know my old house doesn't have air? I'm literally sweating off precious pounds." I had already lost enough weight when I found out how sick my dad was, and I couldn't make it home fast enough. I blamed myself and hated myself. When stress hits, I don't eat, I close up.

"How does it feel to stay in your old room? I couldn't bear to go back to mine. I'd rather not choke on nostalgia."

"It feels, weird." I don't tell him about all the nights I have been spending at the school, with Bryan.

"I like weird. It brings out the truth in us. How's this feel?"

"I told you. Warm."

"Not the water."

"I missed the stars. Everything is quiet here, and maybe it's not all bad. Where do you think you'll end up when you settle down?"

"Maybe someplace like this. Maybe a city. I'm still trying things on. It's nice not to be tethered to anything."

He makes it easy to remind myself that I can't get caught up in that smile. In his voice. Not that I want to be tethered to someone. Or maybe I do. I confuse myself, so the last thing I expect is to make sense to anyone else.

"I love the city. I love to disappear," I say. I miss the sound of horns blaring and voices in the streets. Sometimes silence is too much. My addiction seeking mind wants to fill the void. And maybe that's what I'm doing with Bryan. "Have you ever lost yourself in someone?" I ask.

I hear the water rustling around him. I turn to see if he's coming toward me. He isn't; instead, he's running his hands through his hair.

I watch his skin, the light playing with it. I don't know why I ever thought he wasn't as beautiful as his brother. He may be more beautiful. Because he is untamed. He looks like the sun. Tan skin and a smile that burns you.

"I had a pretty crazy affair with this girl a few years ago."

"Affair?"

"No. Sorry, not the right word. Relationship, I guess. It was like a six-month thing, but it was intense. The kind of thing you think you'll never recover from. But I did. I did, but she's still there." He points to his chest. "You can move on from something, but always have this piece of a person in you."

I envied him. Had I ever had that? No. A high school crush hadn't altered me. It was the fantasy of it. Not anything real. Not anything real between me and Bryan.

"I think that's a beautiful thing to think."

"To know. So, yeah. You love my brother."

"No." I cross my arms over my chest, rise from the water. I'm not surprised by my answer. Teenage Severin always wondered, then convinced herself she was in love. But I knew the truth now. "I've never been in love. Can you believe that?"

"Yes."

"What? Why can you believe it?"

"I don't know. You're all spark. All smart-ass comments and *trying to make up for lost time* and that can lead to the tallest walls around someone." His eyes burn into me.

"You always have all the answers." I splash some water at him to break the spell.

He lets it hit him in the face. "Fake it 'till you make it, that's what I say."

"Can I tell you something without you letting it go to your head?"

"I can't make that kind of promise." He wipes the water from his face.

"Okay. Whatever."

"Spill it."

I confess to him then. All of my loneliness. "You're my only friend here."

He doesn't laugh at me. I expect a joke. Something to make the moment...less. But it never comes. He gives me what I need, not what I want. "You're not my only friend here, Sevvy. But you're the one I like the most."

The moment reminds me of something my sister said once about intimacy. About opening yourself up to vulnerable moments and words that open you up, belly first. I feel so frighteningly vulnerable. "This is weird," I say.

"I can be nice."

"I know," I turn away. "Just don't get too nice."

BOY STUFF

PAST

IT BEGAN SLOWLY. UNEXPECTED. IS IT CALLED AN AFFAIR when you're not married? Is it called an affair, such a heavy word, when you're just a child? I saw him watching me in the halls, at lunch. When I finally had enough courage to look up at him, I saw it. What my friends had been telling me. I saw remorse there. The kind of regret that you can't wipe off your face. But then I also saw his laughter and his lips on Aurora's. I saw their hands and arms and bodies touching. I saw all the ways they clung to each other. Like two people who had been starved for affection, finding each other for the first time.

They were high school royalty. They were the couple who'd been struggling to find each other in the entire movie. And now they were kissing, together at last.

I was forgotten. My crush was forgotten. And I was grateful for that at least. Homecoming was forgotten. And I was able to lurk in the shadows the way I always did.

My friends and I hung out at the Falcon's Nest. We played pool. We ate sour cream fries and had too much Pepsi. We felt invincible. One car between the four of us was all it took. The future was ours. Broken hearts could not stop us.

It was a Thursday, the second day he reached out to me. I went out to Britt's car in the Falcon's Nest parking lot to grab my glasses, and there he was. Parked, sitting, staring at me through the windshield.

I froze, unable to move. He flicked his jaw, motioning to his passenger door.

For a moment I just stared, defiant. I looked at those lips, lips that had been all over Aurora after fifth period. My head moved from side to side, a heavy rejection. I felt it in the pit of my stomach. In reply, he mouthed one word. One word to break me open, to beg me. *"Please."*

I couldn't control my body after that. I walked around the front of his truck, to the door. I climbed onto the side step, peered in his window. He reached over, slowly unrolling it. I let my hot breath leave a mark behind.

"Get in." It wasn't like him to demand. I didn't like it. I shook my head again. "I need to talk to you."

"About what? It didn't go so well the last time, and I think everything is clear between us. Don't feel bad. I wasn't surprised, honestly. We knew where this was going. And there was never anything between us." I was rambling, staring at my white knuckles on the frame of his truck.

"That doesn't mean I don't want to talk to you. In private."

"Can you even be here? There isn't a big red curtain to hide you this time."

"It's not a good idea. No. Please get in."

"I'll have to let my friends know." I pulled out my cell phone and flipped it open. It was for emergencies only. I shoved it back in my pocket and hopped off the truck. I walked back into the Falcon, straight to the pool table. Britt was laughing at something Akia had said, and Christina was rolling her eyes at them, a fry hanging out of her mouth. She stood up at the sight of me. I wondered what she read on my face.

"What's that look? Did someone break into the car?"

I shook my head. "Has any car in the history of Burlingame ever been broken into?"

"Probably not," Britt confirmed, setting her pool stick down. "What's up?"

"Bryan is out there. He's wanting me to go with him. To have a talk."

"No fucking way." Britt's rejection of the idea was immediate, startling.

I reached for my jean jacket, shrugged my shoulders. Like I had no choice. And in my head, I didn't. I would follow him anywhere.

I looked at Christina as I left. She mouthed *I love you* and I tried to smile.

————

We ended up at Bryan's house. A place I had seen, but never thought I would enter. It was located behind the church. Bryan parked in the back. There were no other vehicles around, but I still wondered at the risk he was taking, bringing me there.

I followed him inside, noting everything. The wide-open entryway, the formal dining room to the left, the office to the right. A staircase made of dark wood, and a grandfather clock in the foyer. He took the steps two at a time and my heart thundered in my chest. We were going to his bedroom. Fuck.

I followed him into the room, my hands wringing, knuckles white. The room was clean, sparse. White walls and a navy comforter. A desk in the corner with a small lamp. The window had large white blinds, the expensive kind, not the shitty plastic ones that covered my window. He had his own bathroom. I saw him walk into it, turning on the water, washing his hands.

I walked to his bed, my eyes on everything. My foot started to tap the floor nervously. "I think I'm sweating," I said. Bryan turned off the light in his bathroom and came back into his bedroom.

"What? Are you hot?"

"No. I'm nervous. I don't like being in here." I had verbal diarrhea and I needed to get it under control. I started to fan my face dramatically. I wondered if it was red and splotchy, the way it got when I had to direct a scene in drama class. I was so much better at writing things out.

"I'm sorry. Don't be nervous. I just wanted to talk to you again and not worry about any interruptions. My parents are gone. My brother could be here, I never know." He shrugged his shoulders and rolled his eyes.

I stared up at the ceiling, my heart running more wild when Bryan walked toward me. He didn't come to his bed, instead he passed me. He pulled the chair out from under his desk and spun it around, taking a seat.

"You looked happy today with your friends. It made me happy."

"Oh, yeah?" I stopped fanning myself, placed my sweaty palms on my jean clad knees. "What else makes you happy these days?"

"Can you just know that this kills me?"

"Okay. I know now. You told me." It wasn't like me to talk to him like this. This was the snark and bite I reserved for others. But it felt good to actually be myself with him. I fell back on his bed and groaned, making a show. His comforter was plush and soft. I was surrounded by his scent, this place reserved for him and only him. Had Aurora been in this bed? I'm sure he had already found a way to sneak her up here, too. I heard Bryan moving, pushing his desk chair back in, so I sat up. "What are you doing? I liked you over there. Where I can watch you."

"I know you like to watch me." His voice was changed. I didn't know how I felt about it. He didn't stop moving. I eyed him. Suspicious and visibly annoyed, as he came over to the bed, and sat next to me.

"This is a lovely home you have." I was stalling, panicking.

"Thanks. I've lived here my whole life."

"I know that."

"Oh, yeah. I haven't seen you in church lately."

"My dad has been a pushover. He keeps buying my excuses. I think he just doesn't want to know the truth. He suspects boy stuff."

"I'm boy stuff, huh." He turned to me, brushed the hair from my face.

"Stop that." I pulled away, grabbed his wrist. A mistake. The touch was small, pulling, for both of us.

His mouth was on my neck first. I sighed, relenting. It was the first mouth to my neck. The first kiss anywhere but my lips. The first kiss of acceptance. Of giving in to our many mistakes.

EASY ESCAPE

One month goes by. My father's health is like a rollercoaster, and I cling to my sister. I cling to Ben and his new friendship. It revives me. I lose myself in Bryan. It buries me.

"Did you dance like this with Mom?" I ask my father. It is a day when he remembers. We brought his old record player to the home. My sister is sitting next to it, rifling through the small collection of records we brought here. An Eagles song plays and I dance with my father.

"Yes. Your mother loved to dance." I can't help the happiness in my heart in this moment. I let it swell through me. I let myself have this. It is an easy escape, when everything else looks so grim despite the sun, the warping heat.

The windows are open and I hear the other residents outside. Normally we would be out walking. But my father wanted to dance. And anything he wants, we give him. I eye the pizza box on the tray table next to his bed. We have full bellies and laughing faces. I wink at Sasha when she looks my way.

My aunt is in the corner, tidying things. Stealing looks at me and my father. She looks both sad and happy. I wonder what she feels. How the twin connection pulls at her right then. I bring her into the moment. "Aunt V, did you go out dancing, too?"

"With them?"

"Yes."

"I sure did. Though you didn't want me to, right, Cassidy?"

My father lets go of me, the song ending. "It's hard to dance with your girl and keep an eye on your sister at the same time. I didn't want anyone pawing at you."

"Pawing." My aunt rolls her eyes and I imagine them in the previous century. Young and dancing. Far away from Kansas, where they settled. "You just didn't like any of the boys I wanted to date back then."

"I sure didn't," my father says, walking to his bed. "They wanted to keep you in the shadows."

———

Fucking and forgetting the past, this is what Bryan and I are doing. Secret meetings, and when I'm not with him, I obsess. I stalk his social media. I map his relationship with Aurora. I look at hers, too. I'm a crazy person. I have a treasure in my hands and I'm afraid someone will rip away it from me, so I hold on to every detail. This is my addiction now. This is my focus, my well, sucking up my energy. I ignore the roses being left at my house, on my windowsill.

Bryan and I run through the field in front of us at full speed. I don't remember ever seeing him look so free, so easy around the eyes. Not even in high school did he look this way. It's beautiful and sad. I find the sadness in the way it is brought out. By me. The one who will leave, eventually.

He is anchored now, in a way I never want to be. We reach the barn and the rain intensifies. I'm soaked and he is soaked and I want to see everything inside of him. His cowardly parts and everything vulnerable.

Everything he thinks is not enough. Maybe it isn't enough for me. I don't know how to be seventeen again. Free and looking at everything in rose-colored hues.

There is moonlight shining through the large open window at the top of the barn, above Bryan's head. The water in his hair looks like stars; he is so like the night. I wonder what I want more. This darkness or the light his brother infuses into my chest.

"What if I'm in love with you?" he asks, startling me.

I try to hide it. "What if that breaks your heart?" I walk to him, take one of his hands in my own. "I don't know what's going on in that storm of a head up there any more than I know what that storm outside is going to do. But I know that you can't handle any more heartbreak. You can't handle any more disappointment." It's such a laughable thing. To want to protect the one who has wounded you.

"Maybe it's my turn though." He runs his thumb over the back of my hand, over my veins and the truth of me.

"For what?"

"Payback. For what I did to you. I broke your heart. Now it's my turn to be the one who gets hurt. It's my turn to be the one who loves more. I've never been that person."

"The one who loves more?" I want him to stop using a word he does not mean. He's been in love with one woman for over ten years of his life and he likes this thing with me, because it reminds him of the beginning. I can feel it. The way he wants to fall into me, so he feels redeemed.

"Yeah. You know, I saw where that got my mother." He ignores my questioning tone. I do not stop him when he speaks of his family. I'm tired of only getting insight from Ben, who hides nothing from me.

"Do you think there is always someone who loves more?"

"I do. Yes."

"Interesting." I drop his hand, my mind on my mother and father. Who loved who more? My mother who fell first? My father for being in love long after she was gone?

"So, you don't believe me?" He reaches for my hair, rubs the end of a curl in between his fingers. It's frizzing in the rain. I love when he plays with my hair, when he traces me.

"Believe that you think you may be in love with me? Yeah, I believe it. I believe you would give anything to have something to hold onto. The world has crumbled beneath you. I'm not a lifeline. I'm not a cure for the sadness you have been feeling." I smell beer on his breath again. It was there when I picked him up. I want to know what he is hiding. Who he thinks he can fool.

"I hate when you say things like that. Because then I doubt myself." He walks away, to the edge of the barn. The rain falls. He looks like he is standing behind a waterfall. The illumination is breathtaking. I will write about this moment. I walk to him.

"If you loved me. If you had truly fallen for me, you wouldn't doubt it for a second. And I'm looking for nothing less than that." The truth is, I've never been in love. And I don't know how to say that. I was so lost in the idea of it. And every echo of all my father told me is bubbling up.

"You deserve nothing less than that."

"I know."

"I know you know."

"I like you," he says.

"That," I smile, taking his hand again, bring it to my lips, "that I do believe. And there is nothing wrong with it being just that. Don't force things and don't rush things. And don't forget the other thing."

"It all sounds romantic until I remember that I'm just a stepping stone. Someone to pass time with while you pass the time here."

"This isn't a vacation. Some fun holiday. And you know why we could never work. The other part of that sentence." I think of my day with my father and my sister and my aunt. He is sick. Dancing and laughing cannot hide that. There is a cough that will not go away. I stayed in bed all afternoon, feigning fatigue. Instead, I cried into my warm pillow. I pulled a sheet from my closet and tacked it up on the wall, blocking out the sun. Eventually I was able to sleep. When I woke, I texted Bryan. Telling him I needed him. I ignored a text from Ben. He couldn't give me the particular medicine I was in search of.

"What other part?"

"The reason you have to stay here."

"I love her." He is a good father. This I have learned. I watch them, him and his daughter.

"I know. You make me happy when I need to feel happy, I hope you know that, too."

"I don't think I'm the one who makes you feel happy," Bryan says, as if he can hear his brother's name in my head.

"I know, I know. You say it's your brother. We're friends." The lie doesn't feel nice coming from my mouth.

Bryan's voice is low. "Maybe all good things are built from that."

"And here I thought you hated the idea of him and I even being in the same room together."

"I don't like it. I can't compete with it. With him."

I want to argue, but I can't keep lying. "What do you mean?"

"He's the one who laughs." Bryan sticks his hand into the rain, closes his eyes. "The one everyone loves. Because he just has fun, and he doesn't worry about anything. He doesn't care about responsibility or the future. It was always so easy for my mom and him. He didn't ask her about the hard things. He just laughed and he made her laugh and it was easy."

"That was his way of coping." My sister and I handle things differently, too. She catalogues things, organizes. I find a new obsession. Because I can't sit in a room alone with my thoughts.

"Is that something you're assuming or something he said?" His voice has an edge, so I walk away from him.

I'm pulled in too many directions. My shoulders feel heavy and I can feel a headache coming on. I wish I had time for reassurance. I wonder how my sister does it. How she did it for years. How she could be responsible for her own happiness and mine, too. Always the hand on a shoulder, even miles away. "Listen," I start, "I don't want to get in the middle of this family thing you guys have. It's between you two and I just, I can't get into this back and forth. Things that you two need to hash out yourselves." I rarely have to spell it out for Ben. He doesn't act like the younger brother, in that way.

"You're right," Bryan says, groaning.

"I know I am."

"Doesn't mean I like it and it doesn't mean I'm happy about any of this. Of this situation and the way he takes and takes."

"Try again." I suppress my own groan. I just want to touch him and feel better. It hits me then. Maybe the boy I thought I loved is nothing but my Band-Aid.

"What?"

"Don't be a cliché." I want to get a rise out of him. Turn the blue away.

"I hate you sometimes." He laughs, and it seems to be for my benefit. Almost like a little *"lol"* at the end of a text.

"And here you thought you loved me. Glad we cleared that up." I wrap my arms around his waist, place my ear on his chest. I want to hear him. I want to remember it. I want to write about him in a way that will not wound him. I owe him that. "Do you still carry regret?" I ask, as he rests his chin on my head.

"Over high school?" he asks.

I slip my hands under his shirt. He is so soft. I never forgot that. "Yes," I say. I don't let him answer. "I don't know why I did it. Why I let myself be someone I never thought I would be. And here I am. So it makes me wonder. Was it a mistake? An error in judgment? Or is this just who I am? Forgetting moral rules and just taking what I want?" My father would have been ashamed of me back then. He would be ashamed of me now, if he knew.

"Now is different, though. We are separated. Broken up." He pulls away so he can look into my eyes. I'm not sad, so I don't show him sadness.

"She still has your last name and you're still legally bound. It doesn't seem right." It's the first time I let this wall down. The first time I don't pretend I still hate Aurora because of everything that happened in high school.

"I can't be in purgatory, waiting for our house to sell and for the divorce to go through. I can't just, wait."

"Funny. That's how you have described your entire life here. Purgatory. I guess it doesn't feel like heaven when you touch me?"

"I've never heard you be cheesy. I don't like it."

"I wish you could tell when I'm being a smart-ass." *Ben would have gotten it.* I shrug the thought off. Bryan moans when I kiss him, when I bite his lip. He pulls my hair and it's what I need.

"Fucking hell, woman," he says, when I let him pull away.

"Yeah. I'm more like that, I guess." I close my eyes as he tastes my neck, looking away from the open cornfield, blocking out the past that filled the space under the old barn roof.

I WANT YOU

PAST

"Tell me you're going to end this," Britt said, standing next to my locker after school. Christina and Akia weren't around to save me.

I shut my locker and started shoving my French book into my backpack.

"End what?" I was focused on the jammed zipper, the hum of bodies in the hall. The way Bryan had winked at me in class earlier.

"The Bryan thing."

My eyes shot up to her face. "Shut upppppp." I looked around to see if anyone had heard.

"What?" She shrugged her shoulders, uncaring.

"You want people to hear?"

"Sev. I love you. But it's shitty to do that to Aurora and it's shitty that he is doing that to you."

I flinched at Aurora's name. Why did she care about her? "I know." My voice was low. I knew she was right, but blame was something my friends and I hadn't given to anyone but Bryan, up until this point.

"Where do you see this going? Do you think they will break up?"

I didn't want to answer. I knew the answer. So I said a lie. "I don't know." I walked off, not wanting more judgment. Not understanding why she was so worried about Aurora. Not understanding why I was letting myself be so weak.

———

The cornfields were where we liked to go. The stalks were gone, and Kansas open earth stretched out ahead of us. The Winthrop's red barn sat on the edge, the perfect hiding spot for Bryan's old truck. We climbed to the second story of the barn most Wednesday nights. Bryan told his parents he needed to work on homework, so he couldn't attend church. His grades weren't the best. It was the only way they would let him out of worship.

My father and I never attended Wednesday night services. We were a strictly Sunday morning duo.

I stretched out on the blanket in the hayloft, wiggling my toes. I wanted to sigh—I felt content—but I held it in. I was wary of letting Bryan see me so relaxed. Letting him see how happy these moments with him made me. It was wrong, what we were doing, but it wasn't sordid. We kissed until our lips were raw. He touched me, slowly, deliberately, but I never let him do more than slip a hand underneath my bra. My panties were on lockdown and I didn't see that changing. I was still terrified of sex and I wouldn't let my first time be with a guy who had a girlfriend, no matter how in love with him I was.

He knew that. He didn't press. And the reason he wouldn't, would hit me late at night. When I wasn't near him. Why would he push me for sex when he was getting sex from his girlfriend? I was unsure of his need for me. Their hallway PDA had lessened since I let him kiss me. He seemed pained when I was near. Maybe I made it up, maybe it was real, his shame. It was raining the night I felt daring. The night I decided to question everything.

"Do you love her?" I was staring at the barn ceiling. Bryan was working on biology homework. It wasn't a complete lie that he was studying. Sometimes we would crack our books open when things got too heavy. When things were too heated. Study breaks from studying the breaks and curves of each other's bodies.

I heard Bryan's book close. The shuffling of his body. "I don't know. To me, love seems to be more of a planned thing."

"What do you mean?"

"My parents are all about plans. About mapping our lives. They say God has a plan but we need to busy our minds with one of our own. To be worthy of the one God will ultimately make happen for us. We cannot be idle. Aurora is part of the plan."

"God's plan? Or yours?"

"I don't know. Both?" He lied down next to me, ran his fingers over my knuckles, clenched in a fist next to my body. I clenched tighter.

"What is this then?" I pulled my hand away, crossed it over my torso.

"A mistake I can't stop making." I didn't flinch at being called a mistake. I held it in, the wound. My smart mouth came out more and more with Bryan, though muted and diluted. Now I really bit my tongue.

"I'm never going to fuck you." I said it to the damp air. No bite. No resentment. If he was playing the long game, he needed to know. I would graduate a virgin. I would go off to college. I would fall in love there, and hopefully, forget all of this.

"I know you're not. That's not why I spend time with you."

"Why do you?" I pushed off the blanket, turned to him. His hands were clasped, settled over his stomach. I saw a sliver of skin showing. Pale like the moonlight. He was so soft. I did not touch him.

"I like you."

He offered nothing else. And it was that way with him. Always. Did he offer more to Aurora? Or did she pull it from him? She was pushy, loud. She filled a room and I sunk into the walls unless I was in safe company. I laughed and joked and howled, with my friends, where I felt safe. Aurora seemed to feel safe everywhere she went. Safe to be herself. She was a force, and I was forced into the shadows of this triangle. "If only life were always that simple. If only life let it just come to that and let us have what we want."

He could have what he wanted. That was his life. Easy and giving. He was the open palm, taking. Perhaps the problem was that he had no clue what he wanted. I knew I deserved better but I was savoring moments. Counting down until the moment I left this town. I never wanted to come back and at times I wanted to take him with me. He had confessed he wanted to go to school in Topeka. Just a half hour away. The whole world was out there waiting for us and he wanted to go to Topeka. The same place as Aurora, who didn't want to leave her family and their large open fields, their farm. She was the pretty Dairy Princess. I couldn't fathom that life. I couldn't imagine not wanting more.

"I want you." He went to say more, but the slamming of a car door stopped him.

We both froze, staring into each other's eyes. I heard his name being shouted down below, outside.

We crawled along the barn second story floor, peering over the edge. Ben Winthrop was down below standing next to his brother's truck. "Bryan? Where are you? I need a ride into town."

Bryan rolled over and ran a hand over his face. I pushed into him, my tongue tracing his ear.

"Fuck," he said. "What are you doing?"

It was so easy to get those reactions from him when I knew our time was ending. It was safe. I didn't have to see where things would go, because I knew our time was up.

Bryan poked his head over the side, yelled at his brother. "I'll pick you up at the house!"

Ben yelled back "Okay. And I know who you have up there so riding together isn't an issue."

Bryan shot up, looked me in my eyes. They were wide, and my skin began to grow hotter. I couldn't speak, so Bryan did. "Well, I guess my brother knows I like you."

I smiled at him, through my fear. He said he liked me, again. And in that moment, it was enough.

THROW THE SCENT OFF

"He doesn't like you." Ben's voice is lazy. He yawns, and I want to punch him in his mouth. We are standing in my front yard. I've only been home for a half hour. But he doesn't know I didn't sleep here. Or maybe he does, and he is saving that remark.

He is helping me wash Beau. Sasha has already been outside with a pitcher of lemonade, and I can tell she likes Ben. She likes him for me. And it makes me wonder if this is what I would feel like if I had a mother telling me she liked a boy. If I would immediately find the boy unacceptable for me. Instead of punching Ben, I spray him with water.

"He told me so," I reply. And it sounds weak.

"What did he say?" Ben asks, wiping his face.

I laugh, pissed at myself. "He said he liked me." I grab the towel on the ground and dry Beau off. He stands still. Such a good boy.

"That's it?" Ben winds up the hose, staring over at the school.

"Yeah."

"Well, how about you call me when you decide to stop lying?" The hose goes 'round and 'round his arm, getting shorter and shorter.

I call out when he goes to hang it up on the hook by the house. "Hey, asshole, lay off!" I see the blinds move, Sasha's raised eyebrow.

He turns back. Crosses his arms over his chest, saying nothing.

"Why are you doing this?" I ask. Beau runs off when I pull the towel away.

"It's for your own good. Say it."

"He said '*I like you*'." I stare at my bare feet, at the polish on my toes, hoping Ben will speak, saving me from the rest. But he is silent, waiting, so I look up into his eyes. "Then, he said *I love her.*"

It didn't matter that he was talking about his daughter. There was another truth there. It swells around us. Hot as the air, just as threatening.

Ben nods when I look up, into his green eyes. "He always will, Sev. It'll fade, and it may piss him off. It may ruin any chance for him to get anyone else he wants. But he loves her. It's not healthy, and it's not smart. But fuck, that's love, I guess. It's like that in the movies and the books. So it's gotta come from somewhere. That's real life." I nod at him when he motions to our empty glasses on the porch. I watch his arms as he pours from the sweaty pitcher.

"I've been in love with him half my life, it seems." It's easy to use that word, even though I know the truth now.

"Are you sure?"

"Yeah." I count out loud. "Ever since…"

"No, I mean, are you sure you're in love with him? That's not real, you know. It's a crush. A pretty long crush, I'm impressed. But still, a crush."

"Are you telling me how I feel now?" He isn't wrong, but I'm reaching for something here now. Something inside of him.

"I'm making you question it."

"Yeah, well, you've been doing that for a while." I think of roses, the scent outside my window.

"We should question everything in life."

"Yeah, I guess so." I gulp my drink down, wipe my mouth with my sweaty arm. The heat is already too much.

"Wait, what do you mean I've been making you question that? That in particular?" he asks.

"Nothing. It doesn't matter. When are you leaving town?" We have been talking about our expiration date. It doesn't feel as heavy as it does with Bryan. Ben doesn't make me feel guilty for my inevitable escape. He craves it, too.

"When you leave," he says.

"Oh, yeah? You're gonna stick around until my father passes?" I walk to the porch, set my glass down. It almost breaks. I didn't mean to set it down so hard.

"Fuck," Ben says, behind me.

"Fuck, indeed." I turn to him, eyeing the school, over his shoulder. I have a day date with Bryan later. In town. In front of everyone, if I'm lucky. If we get this right.

"Is that really how long you're staying? Don't you have a job to go back to?" Ben loses his smart-ass tone. He uses the gentle one, saved for these moments only. When I bring up my father. I can speak about him in a way I cannot with others. Not with Bryan. Not with my sister. Not with my aunt. Because he isn't trying to comfort me. He is trying to listen. He doesn't know what it means to me.

"I'm a writer. I can work remotely until I finish the project I'm working on." I haven't been working on anything. When in the face of my muse, it seems, I clam up. Or maybe grief shuts the door. "When it's time to meet with people, shop it around, that's when the face-to-face fun is necessary. I packed up my apartment, sublet it."

"I see. Are you ready for today?"

"I'm not ready."

"I bet. See you there."

Ben leaves me to clean up. When I'm done, I sit on the front porch, staring across the street at Bryan's truck.

Surviving Burlingame means playing games. Cute little games. To secure community funding for the low-income apartments, a fundraiser is going on in the town square. That damn gazebo and that damn town. And I'm going to be there. Because Bryan wants me to go. To be out in the open with him. It's what I've wanted. What I tell him I deserve when we are together, but I'm dreading it. They are auctioning off eligible dates with eligible bachelors. Bryan is not an eligible bachelor, but as I told him, people still care about him. Some people are on his side.

It's scandalous. Burlingame's golden couple, officially out as broken up. As, moving on. In a way.

Bryan is making a statement by putting himself up for auction. I'm unsure of how I feel about it. For his sake. The gossips of Burlingame can be fierce.

I didn't ask what was in his basket, but he winked at me when he carried it out of his bedroom. I yawned around my smile, my eyes sharing his mischief.

Now, my confidence in winning his basket is dwindling.

———

Two hours later, I walk up to the gazebo in the town square, filled with familiar faces I want to avoid.

I spot Aurora immediately. Her blonde locks always stood out. She is five-eleven and always wears heels. She wants the whole world to know where she is in a crowd. At times, I do not damn the way she peacocks herself in a room. I see insecurity behind it.

I look away from her and look up into the gazebo and find Bryan's eyes. They are cold, in a way I'm not familiar with, and don't want to be. I've seen his frustration. His lust. His indifference.

His eyes flitter to Aurora, and I see it. The love and the loss of it. I wish I knew how he felt. But I'm still the novice when it comes to real relationships. Always watching him and his experiences, listening to his stories of their past, when he gives them. Feeding off them.

I laugh, to myself, and there is no humor there. I tug on my sleeveless top, riding up on my shoulder. There is still a burn there, and I feel like walking summer. My skin is hot, but it's not the heat. It's the slow rage building. I'm a dumbass, and I have no one to blame but myself.

When I look back up at the gazebo my eyes catch another Winthrop. Bryan's father has his arm draped over both of his sons, and he is watching me. He saw my eyes all over his eldest. Did he know about our affair in high school? How could I be so stupid? Of course he did. This town is nothing but ears and mouths willing to share every sin. I do not look away until he does. His soft preacher's laugh finds my ears, and I wish I didn't know his every secret. I want to look at him like I did as a little girl. Sweet Brent Winthrop. Town savior. Kind voice and there to ease your worries, forgive your sins. There to hide his own.

I hear a wolf whistle and jump. Ben calls to me. "Sevvy! Girl, you better win my basket." I blush, then turn white when I see Bryan whip his eyes to his brother.

I hate myself.

I hate Ben.

I want Ben sometimes, and that scares the ever-loving shit out of me.

The crowd swallows me when I walk away, from the stares and the noise. I find my tree, close to the courthouse. I can see everything and watch in silence. I run over the winners' rewards. A picnic around the town pond. Perfectly blue and surrounded by yellow flowers. A date at Nelly's Steakhouse, by candlelight. It's like one huge group date. Young and old. Rich and poor. If you have enough cash saved to bid on the basket of the mayor, then you're in. You can do what you want after the town sees you run through the motions. Did many hit it off in real life? My father found himself auctioned off when I was a little girl. My sister and I hoped he would find someone he liked. Someone to come around. Be a mother to us.

My father arrived home by eight p.m. and brought ice cream. He brushed off our questions, said it was a perfectly lovely date but he wasn't interested in changing his life. He loved his routine with us, and it was all he needed.

We tried not to appear too disappointed. Our dreams and plans dashed away by his dismissal of Dorothy, the sweet lady who ran the register at the Town and Country supermarket in town.

She wasn't here when I returned to town. My aunt told me she married the former vice principal and then moved to Topeka.

I could never help my wandering thoughts. My obsessions. Would she have been there for my father had their date turned into more? Would she be visiting him right now? Would she be there for him until the end? The end, I can feel it approaching like a slow-moving train. Just one more thing for me to obsess over. Just one more loss to mourn. A glimmer of hope gone before I could even touch it.

What's worse, having a nuclear family that is toxic behind closed doors? Or having a family that is missing a vital piece? I wish I knew.

I look into the crowd, over to Aurora, and see Britt. She is looking at me, all alone, trying to hide from the crowd. She leaves Aurora and comes in my direction. My stomach lurches.

You need closure in your life. You can't bury the memories. They will always resurface. I thought I pushed all of this down far enough. Now we are all here, open and alive. The ghosts of my past have faces, and they are staring back at me. Reminding me of my sins, past and present.

I will always be the lesser, the one who ran away before her heart could be thoroughly shattered. States and miles cannot cure you of this kind of harrowing shadow. I buried this for years. I manipulated our story, wrote it out, changed the dates and the ending. It's the only way I could stomach it all. The only way I could get through the days, the endless expanse of healing set out in front of me. I took another path. I avoided it. You need closure in your life, and I chose the open wound.

It doesn't hit me, how deeply I buried this, until I see her face close up again. My body reacts. Small tremors, tears shining in my eyes. But I don't let them fall. I can't. I will be strong, and I will keep this spine straight. My chin up, free from the red. I will confront this.

"I guess I just don't see it. How did you become friends? She didn't give us the time of day in high school." I look in Aurora's direction. I think of Britt asking me when I would end it, back then.

"We aren't in high school anymore, Sev. We gotta leave all that in the past. I would think that would be easy for you. You left, and you don't have the reminders. I'm here, where there are old memories everywhere I look, and I left it behind."

"True."

"I guess you didn't though. I mean, you've been writing about this high school crush for years." She looks at Bryan, hard eyes, the same as they always were.

"You make it sound like an obsession."

"But isn't it?" She looks back at me.

"I needed something to focus on. Something to take my mind off what happened. It was just something I did to pass the time. To calm my racing mind. It all just sort of blew up. It wasn't supposed to be the thing that has defined my career so far. I'm going to write something else. I'll write something for her." The silence washes over us. The blame. The resentment. I want to reach out and touch

Britt. I want to hug her. I remember the way her arms felt around me when I was caught up in my own drama. She was a comforter, deep under her forward words, and now she was the enemy by proxy. I break the silence. "I want to go back."

"To what?"

"To cruising around town. To sour cream fries and basketball games. To laughing in the stands and leaning against our lockers, laughing. To crushes. To the time when we thought everything was a tragedy but really, it wasn't. To before everyone started leaving me for good. To when you and I shared things."

"I don't know how to be your friend without messing everything up," she admits. "You said you're not staying. This isn't your home, and I can't throw everything out of whack for someone who never called. For someone who forgot I existed. I get it. You were grieving but so was I. And you all left me at once. I've made this life here, and it's not worth ruining."

"So you can't even choose your own friends now? Sounds like a stellar thing you got with Aurora there." I'm hurting. My throat hurts when I speak, and I don't want to be angry, but it's the only emotion I can let out.

"It's about respect, Sev. You're fucking around with her husband. Yeah, they are separated and all that, but it's still a fact. And they have a kid. A family." She crosses her arms, and her gaze flickers to Aurora. I see it then—their daughter by her side.

Her words hurt me and she will probably brush me off, but I'm not sure I care. I miss my friend. I try out the words. "I miss you, Britt. I don't have many people here."

She stares ahead when she speaks. "You have Bryan. And you have Ben Winthrop, too. Never saw that one coming."

"He's my friend."

"So you have a friend then. Grow up and deal with this."

"You're still kind of bitchy," I whisper. I mean it as a compliment, she doesn't get it. We are so far removed from each other it hurts.

"Sometimes I say the wrong thing. I'm human. But, you wrote it. You put it out into the world. You have to take responsibility for that. Claim it."

"I get it. It hurt people."

"Do you? You wrote it. Own it or don't write anymore."

"I really wish you wouldn't tell me what you think I should do." Jealousy is an ugly thing. And I can hear it beating in my ears, thundering in my heart. I hate Aurora for taking her from me.

"Seriously, Sev, stop being a brat. Just take responsibility for it. Good or bad."

"I missed you, you know? I missed you before I knew you were friends with her."

"I know you want to make her out to be the bad guy. But she has feelings, too. Why are you so easy on him and hard on her? Because it's convenient to forgive him. Forgiving him means you can kiss him, fuck him."

"Fuck him? Or I *can* fuck him?"

"Both, you know I never liked him. He is so shady. He can't figure out what the fuck he wants, so he takes it all."

"Two sides though, right?"

"Maybe. But I say fuck his side. He hurt you, my best friend. And now, whether you like it or not, I'm Aurora's friend. And he's hurting her, too."

"Why does it happen this way? All the damn time. The shitty couples stay together forever."

"They aren't together."

"But aren't they? They're tethered. I can't break him away. He will never want me, and just me, will he?" I'm drowning out the sounds of the crowd. I want to find Ben's eyes. Eyes that always say '*I told you so*' but comfort me regardless.

"I wish I could say yes. Because I know that's what you want to hear. What you've always wanted to hear. But I just don't think so, Sev." She walks away and I cling to my name from her. It sounded like she was talking to a friend for a moment there.

I wipe my eyes and look across the lawn, over to the Winthrop men. Beautiful and tragic. The sound of a booming voice amplified by a microphone pulls me from my thoughts.

What the hell is in Bryan's basket and how can I possibly bid on it with Aurora here? With their daughter here? Talking to Britt has me aching, guilty. I understand moving on, but this would be making a statement that the town would never forget. They still haven't forgotten our transgressions, all those years ago.

My nagging and urging him to move on have hit him too deeply. This isn't what I meant. I meant for him to let the guilt ease from his chest. Not to make some statement in front of the whole town. We both know this is fleeting. Why does he want to let himself sit in the aftermath of this? I can't join him in the blame.

I step closer as the bidding begins on the new high school superintendent.

The men are lined up in front of the gazebo now. A portion of the high school band is playing saxophones out on the lawn. It's so cookie cutter, and it makes me laugh, but it's low. I grew up in a sitcom, and somehow, I forgot. You can't make this shit up, and I never missed it, but I see the charm. I see the safety here. And I get it. You can make a home in a place like this. You can make a home in a person, too. Maybe that's what I'm trying to do.

Bryan is a staple here. He is needed in the grand scheme of things. The town owns him and they love him, even when he falls. I look up at Bryan again, and he is staring at me intensely, so I walk in his direction. I'm always in his gravitational pull.

He walks to the end of the line of men, and I find him. Red face and sweat along his brow. "She brought my daughter."

"I know." It's nearly a whisper. "Did you know she was going to show up? And, I mean, did she even know you were going to do this? I feel like this is something you should have discussed." I feel for Aurora in this moment. Britt is more right than I will let her know.

"I thought you wanted me to do this." His brow furrows, and I shrink a little. Communication is not what we are good at. We are barbs and sex and kissing and hidden desires.

"This specifically? No. I want you to move on and do what you need to be happy. But this seems extreme. And I was too high off the fucking this morning to talk you out of it. I guess it didn't feel real." Talking someone off a cliff when you're post-coital shouldn't be legal.

"Are you kidding me?" I don't like his tone. People are looking at us.

"No, Bryan."

"What do we do?" It's clear, and one of us needs to say it. So I do.

"I can't bid on your basket. I don't even know which one is yours. What's in it?"

"Why? You're not bidding, right?" My neck feels hot, and the tone hasn't left.

"Well, I want to make sure I don't get it."

"Are you going to bid on another one?"

"I was thinking about it." My tone matches his. My lips are a straight line, and I desperately want a cup of coffee. He kept me up all night, and now I wish I had gotten more sleep.

"Are you serious?"

"Yes? Ben said to bid on his."

"That was a joke to piss me off. You're going to?"

"I thought about it. Might throw the scent off?" It's not why I want to bid. I want to feel his company near me. I want to feel something lighter. I want to go back to the feeling of this morning after I left Ben. I didn't dissect it. I didn't scrutinize it when I went inside, even though Sasha started in with a million questions.

"Why do I feel like that isn't the reason you want to?"

It's on my face. My betraying face. Always giving away my emotions and desire. "This again?"

"This. Always. Until it's over."

"Until what's over?" Sometimes our bickering turns me on. Right now, it doesn't.

"All of this." He walks away, leaving me with his anger.

I follow him with my eyes and find Ben's. He's laughing at us.

When the bidding for Ben begins, I raise my hand.

I win.

I'M NOT IN LOVE WITH HIM

PAST

MY FRIENDS ABANDONED ME, CONFUSING MY MUTENESS with acceptance of their retreat. They were traitors, but I had a hard time blaming them.

Aurora took a seat in front of me. I didn't meet her eyes, and she huffed out a breath.

"Hey," I offered, meekly. She was the alpha here. I rubbed the spot behind my ear, remembering the feeling of scissors there when my sister had to cut the chunk out Aurora had stuck gum in as a kid.

"Hey."

We sat in the silence for an awkward amount of time.

"I think you know why I'm here," she said, crossing her arms over her ample chest.

"Yes. I think I know why." I repeated her assumption. She was right. I knew. There had never been a time in the history of high school where Aurora had decided to have a sit-down conversation with me.

"I know you're hanging out with him. And I can assume what's happening, even though he says nothing. You two have never been friends and after the homecoming...situation...I can't figure out why he would want to spend time with you at all if it wasn't to do something more than what friends do when they spend time together."

"I'm not sleeping with him." There was a lump in my throat that wouldn't go away.

"I didn't say you were." She rolled her eyes and reached into her purse, grabbing a cigarette. I didn't know she smoked and it struck me as so basic. So boring and typical. "But I'm sure if he had his way, you would be."

I didn't correct her. It was in the way he looked at me. The way everything stopped, so breathless. He wanted more, and he frightened me, in all his experience. I was a doe in an open field. I was being hunted. I wanted to be captured.

"I'm sorry." I said it, but I didn't fully mean it. I could see in her stare, in her hunched shoulders, that this wasn't easy.

"Are you?" She exhaled, blowing smoke into my face. I reached up and covered my mouth. There was no snap in her tone. It was an honest question that sat on the picnic table between us. I grabbed it.

"Mostly." I placed my head in my hands, gripped my hair. I groaned and straightened. I looked her in the eyes when I spoke again. "I've liked him for two years. And when homecoming happened, I didn't know what you guys were. I didn't know he was going to kiss me. And when the guy you've been crazy about for years finally kisses you, you kiss him back, right? I've hated myself over this but I haven't stopped myself. I didn't expect him to want to hang out again after you two got together and there is no excuse for it, but I like him. I hate that I do and I hate that this whole thing is going on. I don't even know who I am anymore."

"I understand."

I met her eyes again, and the feelings I saw reflected in them made me squirm. "You, understand?"

"I love him. How could I not understand why someone else would fall for him too?" She shrugged her shoulders and stuck her cigarette back in her mouth. I wondered if this was part of her game. To be so calm and collected. To say little, so I would spill everything I knew. It was working.

"I'm not in love with him." I didn't know if I was telling the truth. What was love? I felt like I was too young to feel it. And everything in my life was temporary. I would be leaving this place. I didn't need to fall into anything more profound than this everlasting crush.

She ignored my declaration, snubbed her cigarette out in the ashtray to her right. "Please, please stop hanging out with him."

It was in that moment that I first felt what I should have felt all along. Remorse, true regret. I wasn't riding a high of hanging out with Bryan. I was entirely in the moment. I looked up at Aurora, and her steely gaze was staring over the road, at the town cemetery.

I did this to her. I was a part of this. Was she asking him to stop hanging out with me? Or was that a request she doubted he would honor?

I lost a little bit of it then. My want for him. My crush dimmed, and I wondered if it would shine fully again. How could I be so wrapped in someone who would do this to another person? And more importantly, how could I be that person too?

I nodded, and it was all my coward self could do.

Aurora pressed her long slender fingers to her temple and I had to look away.

I glanced to the right and saw my friends staring at us through the glass of the restaurant. They quickly looked away when they locked eyes with me. Except for Britt. She stared at Aurora.

I turned forward again to the sound of Aurora getting up.

"Okay. Thanks for talking with me," she said.

I sat there for a moment too long after she left. Replaying our words, wondering where my friends were now that they knew I was alone.

I jumped at Britt's hand on my shoulder.

"You okay?" Her eyes were softened. Some of the judgment she felt, high in comparison to others, seemed to fade away before my eyes.

My own eyes were brimming. I realized then that I was shaking. I had been terrified of Aurora. Her vulnerability scared me even more. Perhaps I could have rallied against her anger, if she had shown it to me.

"I think so." My reply was shaky.

My friends sat down around me, quiet. They were waiting for me to fill the space but I didn't know where to begin. Aurora had always been the enemy. She had everything we wanted and was never, *ever* kind to us. We had all grown up together. Played in the playground together. Watched each other through all of our awkward phases and skinned knees and growth spurts.

We were never to feel sorry for her. Never to let her get under our skin. It was a pact we made when we were little. She won all the crowns, and she got all the beautiful boys. In our school, and the surrounding ones. We would give her no pity, and she wouldn't ask for it. She would ask for nothing from us, because we were beneath her. Until today. When she asked something of me.

"I didn't see anyone throw a punch or raise their voices. What the hell was that?" Akia asked.

"I don't know. She, she asked me to stop hanging out with Bryan."

"She told you to?" Christina questioned.

"No, she *asked* me to stop hanging out with him. She asked it, like a favor. Like I had some sort of control over this. And, God, I don't feel like I do. I never have. It's all been what *he's* wanted. We met up when he wanted, and I hated myself."

"What are you going to do?" Christina asked, grabbing my hand.

I felt for her. She was in love with a boy she couldn't have either. She wanted Rodney to be her prom date, but she never asked him. And we were all glad she didn't. We knew what his answer would have been. Sometimes I was pissed at her for still liking the boy who mouthed me that day in the auditorium. "I guess I'm going to go talk to Bryan."

"And you're going to end it?" Britt was hopeful, but skeptical.

She knew I couldn't resist him. He was my addiction and I needed him. I needed him until I left. But prom was fast approaching and I needed to focus my attention elsewhere. I needed to end this.

I didn't reply. I just looked into Britt's eyes.

And she knew.

———

No one tapped on my window. No one but the last person I wanted to see. The one I wanted to avoid, because I knew where it would lead.

I lay in bed for a while. Hoping he would leave.

I had no one to blame but myself, but I wanted to blame him. For everything. For the whole of this high school experience, though that was probably laying it on a little thick.

I huffed out a breath and threw the covers off me. My room was stifling, already.

Bryan's face stared back at me, the moon lighting him up, when I raised the blinds. I knew what he was there for. I knew Aurora had to have told him about our talk. He was here to give me his decision. I was ready for him to say it, to actually say it. Or maybe he would just stare at me, hoping I could read his murky mind.

I opened the window slowly, hoping my father was sound asleep. "What?"

"Can you talk?" He looked nervous. As expected.

I imagined it would suck to break a girl's heart even though you aren't in love with her. All of my wanting made it hard on him. I almost felt sorry for him. The way he had to live his life for everyone else. I would crumble under expectations like that. I didn't answer him. Instead I flapped my hands at him, motioning for him to get out of my way. I climbed into the night even though I had no bra on under my tank top and ugly striped pajama short bottoms on. My legs glowed in the night when I hit the soft ground outside my window. My eyes searched the road; thankfully it was empty.

I saw Bryan's truck parked across the street, so I started for it. Still wordless. My ears burned red with my anger, and humiliation.

I could hear Bryan scurrying to keep up with me. My pace slowed when I hit the pavement. Bare feet were a bad idea, but I just wanted this over with. Done. When I made it to the passenger door I stood there, staring at the handle. I crossed my arms over my chest, suddenly embarrassed that I was out here, so vulnerable.

When I did not move, Bryan reached around me, opening the door for me.

I climbed up and sat down, staring out the windshield, letting him close the door behind me. I barely registered his presence when he got in with me, turning my way.

I could feel his breath on my cheek. Hot and begging me to devour it.

"What is this?" My voice sounded strange. Angry and swollen.

"I think you know."

"She told you she talked to me. You're taking Aurora to prom. You're not breaking up with her." My voice was lifeless. I had little fight in me.

"It's not a good time to hurt her."

"I will be gone soon."

"After the summer?"

"The summer could fly by. What, you're saying you'll do it then? Stop making me laugh."

"Don't be that way. I hate when you're cold."

"Cold?" I reached for his hand, placed his palm against my neck. I was burning up. "I'm filled with so much anger. You have no idea. Do you ever light up with that? No. You're always even. Slow to show anything. I'll be whatever I want to be, Bryan. I am *not* yours. You've seen to that. I'll be cold, I'll be hot. I'll burn this fucking truck to the ground." His grip tightened on my throat a little and I felt myself stiffen in the seat. This was not what I wanted. This wasn't what I wanted to feel.

Sometimes I thought about just giving it to him. My virginity. So I could leave here with some part of him. With some piece of him he couldn't erase with his back and forth. With his constant wavering.

I have never been so sure of a desire. I wanted to claim him and when I felt that want, I thought of my blood. The addiction there. Would I look back and name him my first one?

He was exactly that.

And I needed to resist. Instead of grabbing his face, tasting him, I stared into his eyes. Daring him.

When he made no move, I spoke, pulling his hand from my neck. "My friends hate you." It was mostly Britt, but I didn't say that. "And I'm starting to think they're onto something."

"Oh, they do?" He tried to hold my hand, and I pulled it away.

"Who am I going to ask to go to prom with me? I'm such a fucking idiot. I let you fill my head with this stupid fantasy, that you would take me. I'm so stupid. A stupid little girl." I was starting to get hysterical. I needed to pull it together.

"No."

"Don't try to be my mirror. Some puppet saying what I need. Who the fuck am I going to take to prom?"

"You're really asking me for a recommendation?"

"Yes. It's the least you could do."

"Fuck." He gripped the steering wheel.

I swear, if he tells me he doesn't want to see me with someone else, I will light him on fire. There is no one he can offer me. None of his friends would ask me. None of his friends would let themselves stoop so low. He only stoops this low when the lights are out. When no one can see us. When the town sleeps and we can be hidden. *In the shadows.*

I've fallen into everything my father told me I should never settle for. Everything he never wanted for his little girl.

"Tick-tock," I said, tight-lipped. I wanted a name. I wasn't leaving until I got one.

The air felt stifling in the Jeep. I watched his profile. Watched his window fog, with his heavy in-and-out breath. Finally, he opened his mouth.

"Ben."

"Your brother?" The little Winthrop. He was a year younger than me and Bryan, but the gap seemed to be bigger. Bryan had at least four inches on him. Twenty pounds. "Does he not have a date yet?"

Ben wasn't as popular as his brother, but he still had the Winthrop name. He had his pedigree, better grades, and a wide brace faced smile. Sometimes I would study him. I wondered if he would end up just as beautiful as Bryan.

"No." He was terse. Almost angry. Like I suggested the name.

"Think he would say yes if I asked him?" I sincerely didn't know. I knew the younger brother knew of my relationship with Bryan. I knew he knew who I was. Beyond that, I was in the dark.

"Yes." Again with the barely concealed anger.

"Okay." I reached for the door, feeling his fingers grazing my arm as it left his Jeep, the last piece of me drifting away from him. I scurried across the pavement, faster the second time. I heard his door slam, his following. I had no intention of asking Ben Winthrop to prom. But I would let Bryan believe it.

"Sev!" It was a whisper yell. He didn't want to wake my father, anyone else in the neighborhood.

I turned to him when I made it to the sidewalk in front of my house. I was thankful my father's bedroom was in the back of the house. "What more is there to say? What more can you take from me?"

"Anything you'll give me? It's just not the right time for this. My mother, she is going through a hard time. And this thing with Aurora, as stupid as it sounds, is something she has wanted for me since we were kids. I feel like she puts too much into this, the relationships of her kids, but that doesn't mean I can just forget her feelings."

"Are you kidding me right now? You can't live your life for your mom. You can't live your life for your dad or your faith or your friends. You have to live your life for you. Forget everyone else. Do you think I care that my friends hate you? That my dad would be pissed if he knew we were hanging out?" I wonder if he would always be so filled with guilt. If he would always live his life for others.

"Your dad would be pissed you're hanging with the preacher's son?"

"My dad would be pissed I was hanging with someone who was ashamed to be seen with me in the light of day! He wants more for me than that, and you know what, I do, too." I laughed, shaking my head at myself. "I used to sit at home on Saturday nights and write poetry in this little journal I keep in my nightstand and I would imagine kissing you. And losing my virginity to you. And it all seemed to be this crazy fantasy that I would never be able to live out. And now, now I have this piece of you. And I think the me from like, a year ago, she would have given anything for a piece of you, but that's not enough. I want it all and I shouldn't have to settle for pieces. I will never settle for pieces of you again. Mark my words here, now. I will never fall down this hole with you again."

"Okay. I believe you."

"Good."

"I want to kiss you. I really want to kiss you."

"What? As a parting gift? Save it. Tell me when and where is a good time and place to hit up your brother. That's what I want." I would go to prom alone before I set myself up for another possible rejection.

"I'm sorry, Severin. I'm sorry."

"Give me a good time."

"The whole family is leaving town this Saturday to go to Kansas City. Everyone except Ben. He will be home."

"Okay." I blew out a breath. "Stop looking at me in class. Stop brushing my arms in the hallway. Stop defending me when Rodney cracks jokes. Stop, just, stop being such a coward."

"I'll stop."

"No, wait. Don't do the last one. I'd never fall for a coward. And if you keep being everything I hate, maybe I'll stop falling. I just gotta get out of this town alive."

"I don't want to, but I've been counting the days."

"It'll all be easier then. The choice will be clear. King and queen. Everything will be as it should be." I go up on my tiptoes and wrap my arms around myself, covering my chest. Covering my vulnerability. My armor is wearing down.

"Yeah. Just the way everyone wants it."

"My dad says life is just choices. Roads we take. You can be the passenger, you can let someone take the curves for you, and just hang on. Or you can take the wheel. Take control. I'm taking control. Don't reach out to me anymore. This is done."

"I still want to kiss you."

"You're not in control anymore. You never were."

I walked away, up to my window. I didn't feel his hands on my hips. He didn't help me back up into my room, the ways he always did before. I felt his eyes on my skin, but never his fight. He never had any fight. I wish it hadn't taken me so long to realize what a coward he was. Now, I wondered if I would ever forget it.

WATERCOLOR

I STAND ON THE STAGE, MY ARMS STRETCHED WIDE. "Welcome to the show!" My voice echoes through the auditorium. Ben laughs and takes a seat, watching me.

I came home but I've never felt at home. Not in my old bed. Not walking the streets I skipped along as a child. Not kissing the boy I kissed years ago. I've never felt at home. But here, here I do.

I walk across the stage and the floor complains under my feet. Was it this worn when I walked on it before? It's weathered, weary. I love it. The feel of the sheet hiding the grand piano is rough under my fingertips. I give it a tug, sending dust and dirt flying around. Little bits hit my face and I cough.

"I hope you have your tetanus shot!" Ben calls. I wave him off, running my hand along the slick piano seat. "Do you play?"

"Yes." I step over the seat, lower myself down. My fingers are called to the keys. Maybe this is why I haven't felt at home. I've missed out on doing the one thing I've missed most while living away from my father. He would sing, I would play. Before that it was Sasha. Before that it was my mother.

His voice was smooth, a deep baritone. And our slender fingers were meant to play.

I run my fingers over the keys, leaning to the right, to the left. I don't know if I can play, fully immerse myself in it. I could fall into this. Drown under the memories. Another addiction. Piano classes and late-night learning. It was discarded. Like the rest.

It feels different here. With keys under my hands that are familiar. Keys that shaped me. These and the piano at home, the one I have avoided.

I hear Ben leaving the audience seats. Climbing the side stairs onto the stage.

I'm no singer. I can't belt, but I can carry a tune. I needed to, when I wrote songs. When I wrote for my stories. I begin a song I know, a song I cling to. Blackout.

And it stills him.

I love a good haunting. I want to haunt. For once, I want to be the ghost.

I feel Ben's hands in my hair as I fade out. I lean back, giving in a little. "What are you doing?"

"Touching you."

"Why?"

"Because you're touching me. Maybe you didn't mean to. But you are, with those hands on those keys. You might as well be running them on my skin."

That stops me. The way he is speaking. My hands retreat from the keys, scale my body, and grab his. "Ben. What is this?" I have felt the boiling, the foundation, and all he has been edging toward.

"I'm sorry." His hands pull away, and I fall forward a little.

My neck is warm when I turn around, watching him pace, his large hands stacked on top of his head. I map his figure. Dark jeans, white T-shirt, long hair.

"I like you when you test me. When you make me laugh. When you make things light. I need that. I need this friendship and that release." *I need him, and that thought frightens me.* I needed him back then too, and he showed up.

"And you need a different release, with my brother." He is smiling when he turns around. It's a mask, hiding the rejection. Or the threat of it. Because I'm not sure that's what I was going to offer him.

"I don't know what I need from him. But I need something." I did not need the anger I received earlier. I did not need the shock of Aurora bidding on his basket, taking him away. The crowd cheered, and I turned red. They got what they wanted.

"You need to cross something off a list. Have you?" Ben smiles at me.

"Yes. And yes and yes." I smile back, hoping we are climbing back into familiar territory. Hoping we keep slipping into this strange new space.

"I hope he makes you say that."

"I'm not that vocal." I wink at him, because that is our way, and I don't want him to see inside of me.

"Then he isn't doing it right."

"Isn't it a little weird to want to hook up with the chick who is sleeping with your brother?" *Is it weird that I want to? Who am I?*

"Here's the thing." He plants his hands on his hips, lowers himself to the floor, smoothly. I would have fallen on my ass if I had attempted that move. "There is a lot in life that is only weird because you want to make it weird. Because you analyze it and dissect it and weigh and measure that shit until it's something completely unrecognizable and unenjoyable to you."

"I won't argue with that." When he speaks, I listen. I find myself looking for the argument with Bryan. Always trying to best him. Verbal warfare. With Ben, I'm more open ears and surrender. We spar, but I light up with it. I don't ache.

Maybe that's the rub. I'm looking for the ache. I don't know love or lust without it.

"I'd love to see what you look like with all the shields down." He smiles.

"I don't wear them with you. What would I need to guard myself from?"

"Nothing but the shit you make up in your head. I can see it now. The mental gymnastics."

"But don't you like my brain this way?" I cross my legs, lean back onto the piano keys. They call out.

"Yes." His eyes do not look away.

"Then quit your bitching," I say. "Want to go down to the gym?"

———

"Damn. I danced with a girl here once. And she was damn fine. And I damn near fell in love," Ben says, when we walk into the gym. It is a space in which they have both touched me. I shiver.

"Your senior prom?" I turn around and walk backward.

"It was you, jackass." Ben reaches for me and I slip out of his grasp.

"Shut up. It was a little high school crush. Not love."

"It's funny how you think what you felt for my brother back then was love, but what I felt can't be that. You're the dictator of high school feels. Please, tell me how you determine what's real and what isn't."

"It's different. He and I, we hung out. You and I just went to prom together." I'm glad my friends pushed, guided me.

"Maybe I watched you. Maybe I felt more."

"Are you just speaking in hypotheticals to try to make me come to some realization about how I felt for your brother back then? Or speaking from a truthful place?" The gym is dim, street lights illuminating the space. We did not turn the lights on when we entered. I feel like a trespasser. I wonder when Bryan will be back.

"What's it matter? Is it making you question things?"

Yes. "I'm always questioning things. Right?"

"Right. That you are. It's why I keep you around," he says.

"Did we just become best friends?" I place my arms around an invisible person, pretend I'm waltzing. Ben laughs, and I love it. I love his laugh and his smile. The wrinkles around his eyes and his worn hands.

"We should have become friends a long time ago. Think of all the inside jokes we've missed out on. Think of all the memes we could have been texting each other." He watches my ghost dance, eyes my legs. I feel warm between them.

"Do you think I'm a meme queen? That I like basic humor?" I drop my arms.

"Yes." He smiles.

I chuckle, caught. *He sees me.* "It's true. I so do. I laugh and then I laugh at myself for some of the shit that makes me laugh."

"You don't laugh enough."

"That's not true. I've always been a loud laugher. And I laugh often. But being here, with everything that comes with it..." I don't say it. I don't say my father's name, but he nods. And he knows. "It's a lot. It's this summer heat and all the heavy here. Summers are supposed to be about fun and breaks from everyday life. That's what I think of when I think of days here. The creek beds and walking to the grocery store and sleepovers with my friends. I knew it wouldn't be like when I was a kid, but I didn't know it would be so different. So damn heavy."

He nods, understanding. "I think that's why you call me."

"Because you make me laugh, you make me feel good. Yes, that's why I call you." I admit it. I give him truths. Because he is one of those people I inherently trust. One I believe will give me the truth in return. I want to kiss him, and that startles me. I bring my hand to my neck and I blush. For no one's benefit. It's too dark for him to see, thankfully.

"You're too charming for your own good and I don't like it," he says, walking toward me.

I do not retreat. Not this time. "Nah. I'm not. This is just how I am," I say. What he finds charming, Bryan finds challenging. That is the difference between them. I can be the same woman, and they read me differently. Maybe I behave differently, too. Who am I myself with? I know the answer.

"Yes. Charming," he says, reaching out, pinching my cheeks.

"A baffoon." I stick my tongue out.

"Who even uses that word anymore?" He laughs.

"Me. I like using weird words." I shrug. "Or words most people don't. It was a game my sister and I used to play. Here. And in New York. Sometimes, in LA I would call her up and we would play it on the phone. We would just try to insert random ass uncommon words into conversation. It calmed me down when I wanted to bounce off the walls."

"Well, when my parents would argue, Bryan and I would play hide and seek outside. I know that isn't original or anything, but it always calmed me down."

"We were lucky, you know?" I would have been lost after high school without my sister. Lost in the darkness I left with. I have yet to say his name since I returned. I have yet to say hers. I can feel it bubbling up. I can feel it ready, just below the surface. The name of my pain.

"How so?" Ben asks.

"We had older siblings who loved us, who tried to make the home things better. I know your home thing was worse than mine, but still. They tried to help because they love us. He loves you."

"I know that. A lot of siblings aren't close. I wish you wouldn't push it." He doesn't sound angry. He tells me what's on his mind. He doesn't make it a game. I don't have to pull and pry it from his mouth.

"I'm not trying to push, I just want to make sure you don't do something you regret."

"I know all about regret and family estrangement, thank you. We don't hate each other." His shoulders go up and down. No worry over the animosity between them. As if he can change it with just one word. As if he holds all the power. And maybe he does. What a strange thing.

"If I bring either of you up to the other, you both clam up. Or get mad."

"Have you ever thought about why that is, Sev? I know I give you shit and say he doesn't care about you, but he must. He must care about you. And what is this that we are doing?"

"What do you mean? Don't blame me for this shit." My words have a bite. I open my ears, listening for car doors. For approaching feet.

"I'm not saying you are the reason he and I have animosity. But take credit for your part in it. I was the skinny kid brother and I posed no threat to anything he wanted before. But I'm not that little kid anymore. Why are we spending so much time together?"

"Because you're my only friend here," I state. I think of Britt and our moment together earlier. The hint of her old voice, at the end.

"And?" He is still, and I'm pacing.

"And what? Don't go fishing."

"I wouldn't dare."

"You're being boring, a cliché. You know how I feel about those." I use words that would wound Bryan, or just piss him off. I don't know what I hope they will do to Ben.

"You're so rude sometimes and you don't even care. I used to like it. I'm not sure I do anymore." This is the first time he sounds like Bryan. I don't want his anger, any push back. With Bryan, I know I have some power. Long sought power. Maybe I am riding that high. With Ben, I know he could pack up and leave this town in the blink of an eye.

"Listen. I like you, Ben. But this is all temporary, right? My time here and all of it. Even whatever's happening between your brother and I."

"Ah, yes. Temporary. But the feelings will keep going and what happens won't disappear. If it's all going to just disappear into thin air, just say it." His voice is a dare. I want to taste it.

"Say what?" I push back. Unable to give in. Not yet.

"How you feel," he says, rolling his eyes.

"I like you both, okay? Is that what you want?" I throw my hands up, dramatic, unafraid of the way it makes me look. I shiver and wonder what my body is telling me. If Bryan is nearing.

"Is the conversation with him stimulating? Or is it just other things that are stimulating?"

"The conversation...it's like a game. Some strategic thing. We are both always trying to come out on top, I think. And honestly, I'm not even sure he knows he is playing." I feel like a traitor. Giving away the secrets of our time together. The secrets of my time with Ben are ones I never give up. Not even to my insistent sister. Not fully.

"Trust me. He knows what he is doing. He always does. Even when he is playing the victim."

"Playing the victim?" I lower my eyes. An empty beer can is sitting in the middle of the gym. I kick it. The sound echoes.

"He does that. The tortured stoic thing. It works so well for him. He doesn't say much because he doesn't have a lot to say. There's not a lot going on up there." He points to his head and smiles, wide.

"God, you're a dick. You don't say that to him, do you?"

"That he's stupid? Only if I'm really pissed off." There is a laugh in his voice.

"Don't. Seriously. He is sensitive about it. He thinks he is stupid." I remember grading his papers, our study sessions in the barn. I remember the way he would lower his eyes when I read his English essays. He isn't stupid, but his strengths do not lie where mine do.

"You fell for it, huh? He just wants someone to stroke his ego."

"No." I'm unsure. My voice betrays me.

"You said it was a game. He knows he is playing. And he is winning, clearly." He laughs, his shoulders hopping up and down. It's a pitiful laugh. I don't like being pitied.

"Are we playing a game?" I motion between us.

"Nah." He shakes his head.

"Then just say what you want to."

"I like you."

"And?" I'm waiting for the punchline. For the second act.

"Nothing more. There is no trap. I like you. That's it. I have for a while. Most girls would want me to say it romantically. Like, I've been pining over you since prom night and I thought about you every day since you left. But that's not true and I will not bullshit you. I had a big crush on you when I was a teen and from time to time... I thought of you. When I came back here, I wasn't expecting to see you and when I did, I felt this tumble. What do they call it? Butterflies. Yeah. I felt that. Or maybe moths. They were pretty strong," he smirks.

"This all sounded good until you said you had moths in your belly." I bring my hands to my eyes and cover them, block him out. Blocking out his height and his broad shoulders. His long hair and the stubble on his face.

"I'm a romantic. Through and through."

"Fuck. I don't know what to do with this now." I drop my hands and groan. I want to go to sleep. I want to talk to my sister.

"Just don't hide from it, I guess. Say what you think and don't worry about who it's going to hurt. People are always so worried about pulling the Band-Aid off, so they choke on their truths, let lies spill out."

"Stop being so poetic."

"You give me them good moth flutters, Sevvy."

I laugh, and it feels good. "I don't know what I would do without you here. I don't know how I would make it through all of this. I just want Sasha, and my aunt, to be as happy and calm as they can be. I don't want to lay my burdens on anyone, so I have to put on this act. But you let me talk about anything."

"I never want to burden you. Unburden yourself, remember. We can run to that damn creek again if we need to. And the thing with my brother, fuck. I know he is hurting. And you think I hate him. And maybe sometimes I do. Because he was handed everything good in this life. He was the first, and he was the most loved, and I made them laugh but they wanted the world for him. Or their version of what the world should be. Maybe it's that I pity him. I feel so much pity for him that I can't even be mad anymore. It's washed away. And you think I'm jealous. But, the way you feel for him? What you have? I don't want that for myself. I don't want that from you. I like what you feel for me and the way you treat me. I like sparring, and I like laughing, and I don't want this tragic, desperate drowning thing you cling to. That so many people think they need to cling to. I like this because it's easy and what's so wrong with that?"

"Nothing, I suppose." Maybe I am dramatic. Maybe I do make everything too hard.

"I bet your mom and dad had an uncomplicated love. He always waved to the teachers and laughed outside his bus before the kids piled on. He was one of those people with laugh lines around his eyes, and you knew when he was stern. You respected him, and you just knew he was someone you could come to."

I squint my eyes at him, then it comes back to me. "He drove you guys to a lot of out of town ball games."

"Yeah. He did. I wish you weren't losing him."

"Most people would be careful with those kinds of words around me."

"I'm not most people, and I'm not going to treat you with kid gloves. You don't want that, right?"

"No. Not from you."

"I can read you. You're not as easy as others, but it's there. The set of your jaw and the way your nostrils flare a little. Your skin takes on different shades of pink and red."

"I'm not a watercolor," I chastise.

"But aren't you?"

"I miss the barbs." This is too much.

"Let me be serious with you."

"Okay."

"Okay." He waits a moment. "I'm sorry you had to come here to say goodbye. I'm sorry my family has been throwing wrenches in your life along the way, too." I let him hug me then. I place my ear on his chest and look around the gym. I remember the last time we were here, touching like this. Well, not quite like this. But dancing, my eyes searching.

"I want to feel better," I say. I think of ways to feel better. Ice cream. Creek beds. Air conditioning. All ice. I'm tired of the heat. Ben pulls away, his hands wrap around my elbows and I stare at his chest. At the rise and fall of his T-shirt. My hands are on his hips. We stand like that for a while. Wondering who will move first. I do.

My hands move slowly up his stomach, to his chest. I listen to his breathing. I feel it with my palms. I keep my eyes trained on the key hanging from his neck, then his hands move, too. They are on my hips now, a loose grip. He is waiting for me. I grip his white T-shirt, hear him let out a breath.

"Do it," he says.

I push out my bottom lip, tilt my head back. His green eyes are dark, and he is flushed. I like the way it makes me feel, so I push up on my toes. He is too tall for me to reach, so I need him to let me have this. I need him to realize this could be over in a second. I could take this invitation away.

When he kisses me, I know I will write about it. I know I will make poetry of him and write this moment into a fictional tale. I will hide this in plain sight. My writing gives me away, but I can always lie. Say it was fiction. I can lie and pretend this means nothing. I can even lie to myself.

HIGH ON OREOS AND HEARTSICK

PAST

It was getting hotter. Spring was coming but I felt summer close by. I felt our time coming to an end. I felt my fate staring me down. Prom. Alone. Because I had gambled on a boy who wanted nothing more than to keep me in the shadows. The side girl. The afterthought.

My friends had dates. They had dresses. They matched. The photos would be beautiful.

My dress was hanging on my closet door. Pale yellow, tulle. My hair was going to be down, long waves along my back.

I remembered Bryan's hands there. The way he spoke. *I want to kiss you. I really want to kiss you.* I didn't let him.

I wished for it, too. At night, I prayed for it.

"So, are you still holding out? You need a date. You can't *not* go to prom. We have been waiting for this our entire lives," Britt said, pouting.

"I thought the thing we had been waiting our entire lives for was graduation, so we could leave this town," I said, pushing that night Bryan and I ended away. Pushing away the image of myself crying into my pillow.

"That, too." Christina laughed. She wanted out more than any of us. She was an only child, living with her grandparents. She had few ties. We were her family, more than anything.

I leaned against my locker, slid down. The halls were thinning and we were lingering. We did that now. Now that we didn't have to ride the bus. "Remind me of my options. Again. I'd love to be more depressed than I already am. God."

Britt took a seat next to me, pulled a notebook from her backpack. "I made a list. Remember!"

I smacked my hand on my forehead and she laughed in return. Britt and her lists. I grabbed the notebook and stared at the top name. Blinking. "Has this name always been on the top of the list?" I thought of Bryan and his suggestion. Was this a joke? I had no intention of showing up at the Winthrop's house when I knew Ben would be alone. I had no intentions with him at all.

"No." Britt was smiling.

I looked around my group of friends. They were all smiling. Some secret had been passed between them. While I was wallowing, they were plotting. Always plotting. "I can't ask Ben Winthrop to prom." It felt like a betrayal, even though Bryan put it in my head. It would look like I was trying to get at him, to everyone else. They wouldn't know the reasoning behind it.

Ben Winthrop, the junior. The wild Winthrop. The one you never would have guessed was the preacher's son. The one girls should run from, even though they never had a chance with him.

He played baseball, never going past middle school with the sport his older brother excelled at. He had been dating the Junior Class Prom Queen candidate, Stacey Combs, since the beginning of his sophomore year. They had broken up last week, after rumors of Stacey cheating. Stacey had a prom date. Her rumored other man. Ben, did not have a date. I knew that because of his brother.

"Why can't you ask him? He doesn't have a date," Christina argued.

She had a point but that didn't matter. He wasn't on a pedestal. He wasn't as beautiful as Bryan, but I felt an advantage, due to my age, and the knowledge that he was dateless, but that's all I had. My confidence was shit when it came to Winthrop boys. "I don't think I can take any more rejection at this point. Especially from one family. That's a bit much." My friends exchanged looks, smiles playing against my doubt. "What?"

"What if we knew something you don't?"

Did they know Bryan told me to take him? I never told them, but my friends had ways of finding things. Uncovering secrets. "What?" My body tensed. I sat straight, my spine a vertical line. Akia dropped to her knees in front of me, threw her backpack in my lap, and made a pillow of it. I played with her hair, it was a habit, and pulled a strand of my own into my mouth. Another habit.

"I heard him getting into a fight with his brother the other day. And I heard your name," Akia threw out, casually.

"What were they saying?" I looked down into her amber eyes.

"I don't know, honestly. Something about 'fucking things up' and 'liar' and then they started arguing about their parents so I walked away. Because that seemed like too much to listen in on. I don't want to think the Winthrops have anything but the perfect marriage. It's too weird."

"So what exactly am I supposed to do with this info? This doesn't seem like a good reason to ask him to go to prom with me."

"We just think," Britt said, pulling my eyes to her, "that they seem to be in disagreement when it comes to you, in some regard. So maybe he would go with you just to piss his brother off."

"Wow. Romantic." I moved my legs, motioning for Akia to get up so I could rise off the floor. I was ready to go home. Ready to end this shit week and this shit day and all of it.

"C'mon, Sev," Britt's voice trailed me as I walked down the hallway, to the door. "We all need to go to prom together."

"I don't actually need a date, you know," I threw back.

"I know you don't but you said, just last week, that you wouldn't be caught dead walking into prom alone. That you would rather stay home."

"Don't trust the things that come out of my mouth when I'm high on Oreos and heartsick!" I pushed the double glass doors open, walked onto the green lawn of Burlingame High. We had planned to grab food after school, but I was too tired of keeping up appearances. I could see my little house, just across the street; inside was my little bed and my little fan. My little notebook and my little bowl that only I was allowed to eat cereal out of. I needed those little things.

"Just consider it," Christina called. "Are you not going to the Falcon with us anymore?"

"Nah." I whirled around, showing them my smile, letting them know I wasn't mad or irrational. I was just drained and over the world.

When the world gets to you, you have to take time for yourself. My father said solitude and quiet reflection are needed to heal.

And I needed to heal.

———

Ben Winthrop didn't have a car. He rode to school every day with his brother. Sometimes I saw them arrive. Two silent boys, the younger jettisoning from the vehicle before it barely made it to park. My observations of Bryan meant that I couldn't avoid seeing Ben. He was just, there. A blurry figure in the background, white noise.

Two days later, he stood out to me. It was unavoidable. He stood in front of me after my last period, in the hallway, with a bouquet of roses, pale yellow, so I took notice. I couldn't avoid it. I knew it was a setup, something my friends had organized, but I stopped caring. I stopped trying to avoid their latest plan.

"What's this?" I asked, voice low, reaching for the roses.

"Can we talk outside?" Ben had a raspy voice, lower than his older brother's.

His hands looked larger than Bryan's and maybe he would be taller. I nodded my consent and trailed him. I was afraid to be seen with him. It hit me suddenly. The way I felt like I was doing something wrong. Betraying Bryan in some way, when he had no say-so in my actions. "What's up?" I tried to sound casual when we made it to the front lawn of the school. There were a handful of students left lingering. I felt their eyes on the bouquet in my hands. On me.

"Do you have a date for prom?" Straight to it. No build up.

"No. And I think you knew that already."

"Yeah." He smiled, almost shy, and maybe the braces had something to do with it, but his act, the 'I'm a shy guy' thing was not convincing enough. He had a hard jawline and it was incredibly attractive.

"So is this you asking me to prom?" I didn't want to mince words. This was a setup and I wanted to complete the transaction. I wanted the deal to be done, to move forward. Always forward.

"Yes."

"Okay."

"Okay?"

"Yes. I'll go to prom with you. I already have a dress. It's yellow." I looked at the roses, curious about what else my friends told him.

"I'll make sure I match."

ALL-CONSUMING

We have been here before. I'm doomed to repeat the mistakes of my past. My father would be ashamed of me. What would my mother think if she were alive? Would she understand? Would she have broken all the rules to be with my father? I'll never know.

I'm sitting on my front porch in one of two white Adirondack chairs. A sweet tea sweats on the table next to me.

Aurora's vehicle is large. A white suburban. I expected this earlier. I wonder how their auctioned off date went. I haven't heard from Bryan since then. He is avoiding me and I'm avoiding the truth of what they are. The king and queen. His crown may have fallen, but that means nothing. He will find it again.

His queen has pale hair—it's nearly white now—and tan skin. She has a pink dress on. Typical.

I stand and walk to the edge of the porch. I clutch my glass to my chest. I need something to keep my hands busy. When she makes it to the halfway point of my walkway she looks up, and she smiles. It looks strange on her face. I've never seen her smile aimed my way. It's not a full-mouthed smile. It's not even a real smile, but it's a smile. I don't mistake it for an olive branch. Sometimes predators laugh before they eat you alive.

"Hi." I offer a smile of my own. It feels unnatural on my face. I back up when she ascends the stairs, brushing past me. Her purse smacks into my thigh and I smile a real smile. This feels right.

She takes a seat, sets her purse on the porch. I follow her eyes, staring at the school. I wonder if Bryan is watching. If this is for show or if she really has something she wants to say to me. I walk back to my seat, lower myself down slowly, to my fate.

"I'm sorry to just drop by. But it's not like I have your number or can find you on Facebook. Trust me, I've tried."

"It's okay. I figured it would come to this eventually." We don't have an audience. My friends aren't here to stare through a grimy restaurant window. My only friend left here is now her friend. I have lost.

"Again."

"Again." I feel ashamed. Again. Mistakes repeated and my face lacks remorse. I hide it deep down.

"I'm sorry about your father."

"Thank you." My hand comes to my throat. I feel red and raw. This, I was not expecting. I expected the old Aurora. But she seems different, where I'm the same in many ways.

"I know you didn't come here for what you've found. But you found it, again, nonetheless." There is exhaustion there. She wrings her hands and I wonder where their daughter is. If she is with her father.

"Yes, I did."

"Why? Why is it always this? Why always him? And then you wrote about him and it was humiliating. Do you have any idea how it felt? We moved on and we built something. Then that movie came out and it was a reminder. A reminder of everything here. That he cheated on me and I was the idiot who forgave him. And it wasn't like you wrote me in a favorable light." Her voice is rising.

I'm glad Sasha is already gone. At the home. I'm supposed to join her soon. "Everything is exaggerated in writing." It's not a lie. I made her character crueler. Stupid. A caricature of her.

"You made me a ditzy blonde asshole." She isn't wrong.

"You WERE a blonde asshole who slammed me into a locker once and hissed at me. I know your friends, at your demand, wrote 'Severin is a Slut' on Britt's car after prom."

"I had nothing to do with that. I didn't come up with that idea."

"But?"

"But I didn't discourage them when they said they were going to do it. What did you expect? I was eighteen. You were eighteen too and had no problem fucking my boyfriend."

"I never fucked him."

"But you are now. You're fucking my husband. Does the fact that you wouldn't give it up back then still make you feel good?"

"Yes. It does, actually."

"Does the fact that you're fucking a loser make you feel good?"

"And how is he a loser? Pick a side, Aurora." I'm suddenly angry. Angry at her for talking about him that way, and I know it's unfair.

Bryan can blame her for trapping him here. For giving him a child, something he too often equates with chains. Yet, I feel anger over her unkind words for him. I regret it. My knee jerk defense of him.

"He can't even drive." She stands, pushing the chair back against the side of my house.

"What are you talking about?"

"He got a DWI. Like two nights before you showed up. He can't drive."

I hear ringing in my ears. My vision goes dark, then light. I grip the armrests. My knuckles go white and I find myself putting my head between my knees. I hear movement. Aurora retreating. When I look up she is standing at the edge of my porch, one foot on the steps. She is facing me and her temple is leaning against one of the large beams holding the roof of our porch up. She doesn't look happy, or smug. She looks resigned. Resigned to loving someone who strays, who makes mistakes. Who lives in a black hole.

"Thank you." She knows what she is telling me. She knows the damage. She knows what can and cannot survive this. She can survive this. They can. He and I, we don't have a chance. He doesn't have a chance with me. With her words, I felt my heart crack open.

The past has a funny way of finding us. It should be no surprise. When you run wildly into your old mistakes, you're bound to get hurt.

I watch Aurora turn. I watch her walk down my driveway, to her vehicle. I watch her drive away, because I need to focus my attention on anything that is not the school sitting across the street. My eyes flutter and I blink into the summer sun. The blinds of Bryan's bedroom window move, sway. Or maybe I'm swaying again.

My cell phone starts ringing in the house. I ignore it, pinching the bridge of my nose. I don't believe he will walk over here. He never does. Because that is the way of us. I go to him. I bend for him. He remains still, letting us break all over him. It must be so easy. To be unmoving.

He is following in the footsteps of a fool. I hate him. I hate him and his ignorance.

————

That afternoon, Ben shows up on my doorstep just as I'm leaving to see my father. He asks to come with me, and I accept. I won't avoid him because of the kiss. I won't avoid him the way Bryan is avoiding me.

When we arrive I do not find my sister. I find the staff staring at me with blank faces. I reach into my purse and grab the phone there. The one on silent. I see missed calls from my sister and my aunt. My knees buckle and before I can hit the floor, Ben grabs me.

"Whoa. What's up?" he says, pulling me up.

I stick my phone into his hands, grip his wrist. He takes it from me and thumbs through my text messages. There is nothing there I care to hide.

I feel his hand on my elbow. I do not feel my feet and legs beneath me. I do not feel my body and my knees bend, as my head ducks. I do not hear the passenger door of my car shut behind me. I do not hear the engine start. I do not feel the pressure of Ben's arm behind my seat as he backs my car up. The miles between Burlingame and Topeka are nothing today. They are nothing and I feel nothing inside of my chest. My hands are numb. They do not grab my phone. My mouth does not voice the question I need answered. The question I do not want to ask. Is he dead? Is this over? Is my life now before and after?

We reach the hospital and I feel like seconds have gone by. I stay still, and Ben gets my door. He takes my hand, pulls me up. This is care, and I note it, in my stupor. When we get inside he takes care of everything. He knows my father's first name. He knows what to say and my fingers are interlaced with his. He leads me down the hallway and when I see my sister, he passes me off. Not because he wants to be done, but because he knows what I need. Sasha embraces me and I feel it then. The tears. White hot and blinding. I let myself go, no longer worrying about the pieces she will have to pick up. I feel more arms around me. My aunt is there, too. We lean against the wall. Huddled and holding on.

"He's gone." My sister says and I wish she didn't. I wish for silence and this moment to go on forever. But you cannot run from things. My father taught me that. I just never listened.

When I see his face, his eyes are blue, the lids so full of veins and coldness. He had a stroke. This morning. While I was wallowing in bed, telling Sasha I would be there soon. He had a stroke and died while I was dealing with drama and my messy relationships.

I take his hand and feel some warmth. I feel warmth and the heavy presence of the other people in the room. Ben does not come in. I do not want him to. It's as if he can read my mind, in the heaviest moments. Maybe he is better at all of this, better than I am, and he can teach me.

My cross-body purse is cutting into me and I feel a vibration. I reach into my purse and pull my phone out. I see Bryan's name and I feel sick. I do not want to see him. I do not want worry that comes too late. I do not want apologies that come too late. I do not want his sorrow and his bullshit. Everything he thinks runs and ruins his life, is a blessing. If only he would see it that way.

I throw my phone across the room and I wish then, that I didn't have a heavy cover on it. My sister yelps and my aunt curses, startled.

"I'm sorry," I say, and I'm startled by my voice. It sounds foreign. I don't know what I'm sorry for. For feeling? For showing it?

————

Later that night I ask my aunt about my mother and father. "Were they in love like the movies?"

"What do you mean?" My aunt turns, the dinner plate in her hand covered in soap. She cleans when she grieves. When she is sad and has nothing to say.

"That all-consuming love? The kind they write in novels." I'm eating ice cream. I haven't eaten all day and I feel dizzy. I need sugar and comfort. My sister has locked herself in my bedroom. I told her I would take the couch.

"I guess." Her answer deflates me, she reads my face and sighs. "I'm sorry. It's been...what is it you're wanting to know?"

It's been a long day and although we all knew it would come to this, we didn't think it would be so sudden. We expected more of the same. The slow fade. I don't know which would have been worse. "I don't know. I just wish I had soaked up more, when he could tell me more. It wasn't enough. And then I was scared. Scared to make him relive it. I just wish I knew what a love like that felt like."

"Have you ever been in love?"

"I was in a relationship once." The words fall out. A default answer.

"That doesn't answer the question."

"I don't know. And that's an answer, huh?"

"Yes, it is." She finishes with her plate, then wipes her hands on her apron. The sound of our old wooden chairs being dragged across the linoleum is the only sound in the room when she comes closer. "Your father and your mother had a great love. One filled with ups and downs, like any couple. When it's real, you weather the storms and not everything is the kind of thing you find in the movies. It's brutal and terrible at times. It's steady and comforting. It's everything, and I'm lucky your father married a woman I considered a sister. I'm lucky my brother found his other half. Because so many don't. When you find that, you'll know. It's this thing that hits you deep in your gut. You don't outgrow it and you can't outrun it."

"All-consuming."

"You're going to have that."

"I'm not worried about me. I just think I'll worry about my dad, forever. Even now that he is gone."

"Don't you worry about him. He lived a full life and he loved fully. He loved you and he was loved and not every person has that. We need each other now and every piece of his past we can offer, you and I both know, he was grateful for it. Even when he couldn't say it or didn't remember us."

"How do you stop worrying about the people you love?"

"You never do."

"Did you ever have a love like that? All-consuming?" My aunt never married. Never had children. She traveled after the devastating breakup, the night we don't speak of, taking photos of beautiful places I wondered if I would ever see. I loved when she would come by when she was back home, in Kansas. We would gather around the table in front of me. She would fan photos around, a kaleidoscope of color and a window I desperately wanted to crawl through.

"Yes." She smiles, the wrinkles around her eyes are beautiful to me. And she is the kind of woman who would agree. Who sees the beauty in all the miles we walk. "I've been in love with the world since I was a little girl. I loved changing schools every year or two, unlike your father. I met a man in Spain. Before you were born. Back when I logged a lot of miles."

"Short lived?"

"Yes." She reaches for my hand, squeezes it. "And all-consuming."

"Who left?"

"I did."

"Do you think he forgave you?"

"Yes. And whoever you're going to leave. They may not forgive you. But I know this. You're not meant to stay here. You don't have roots, not in the traditional way. You want to paint the world. And to give that up for love, is to give up the love you have in your heart, for yourself."

"I think that's one of the biggest tragedies in the world." I wring my hands together, stare out the kitchen window.

"What's that?"

"Two universally different people, with vastly different desires, falling in love. Because you can break yourself apart trying to fit into a mold for someone else. You can sacrifice your soul and barely notice until it's too late."

"Do you know how lucky you are? To know that? You're ahead of the curve. You know something about yourself that many people take years to figure out. That many know, but push down, because they can't give up their addiction to someone else."

I flinch at the word. Addiction. "Maybe they aren't all bad?"

She reaches through my vague words. "I don't know. Maybe not all addictions are bad. Maybe they are. That's for you to decide." She pauses. "There is so much of your mother in you. The good and the bad. The empathy, the open mind, and the ears that are always listening to the other side. And your sharp tongue. I see it in your writing, in the women you write."

"I'll never lose that." I vow it. I vow to always be the challenge. To my own detriment, if I must. Just to never give it up.

"Good. And never stop looking."

"For?"

"The other soul you're missing. The one who has no desire to place chains, to put out fires."

"Maybe you should be a writer."

She laughs at my reply, throwing her hands up and rolling her eyes. "I tell my stories through pictures, with my camera. That's my pen."

"It's a lovely one." I look over her shoulder, at the framed photo of my parents on top of a mountain in Ireland. My aunt was there. She was there. She caught that moment.

———

After everyone goes to sleep I walk outside, hoping Bryan will somehow be there. By magic. Or maybe he can feel my mourning. I want to tell him I know what he has done and what that means. Instead, I find Ben. And all my anger and pain is a tight knot in my gut.

He is standing on the sidewalk, staring at the moon. It is white and I feel hot. I walk to him, turn, and stare into the sky. He tries to take my hand and I pull away. I look up at him and he looks wounded, so I walk away. To town. To the city limits sign. I don't know where I'm going. I just need to leave his presence if he wants to give me his pain. Because I have no room for it. We kissed, yes, but that doesn't mean he can take my hand. Make this into something. I'm too raw.

I hear him following me, so I address him over my shoulder, never stopping. "You think I care that we kissed?" *That it knocked me off my axis? Wrecked everything I thought I wanted?*

"Yes. You do. It made you unsettled."

"Maybe I like being unsettled. Maybe that's what I need in life. To be unsettled. So I have something to write about." Ben catches up with me, his fingers graze my elbow, and I stop.

"Don't freak out. I'm sorry. I wanted to take your hand because that's what friends do for their friends when a parent dies. And they hug them and they are there for them. I know maybe you need to be angry right now. Or you need to fight. And honestly, if that's it, then fine. Fight with me."

"Do you know how it feels to have every memory with someone stripped away? To watch their eyes and search for recognition, and find nothing? I need him, and he can't lift me up. He can't help me with this. Because the thing I need help with is mourning him. He was there for me the last time I mourned. He was there when I didn't know what to do with myself and he let me decide, when I figured it out. He didn't argue. His silence and steady presence got me through it. What do I do now?"

"Let's get drunk." Ben says it simply. Not as a joke.

And it is the best idea I've ever heard in my life. I stare into his eyes and my mouth starts to turn up. "Okay."

"Okay."

"No cars." I purse my lips. Try to keep the tears inside.

"Never," Ben replies.

MOSTLY THE ALCOHOL

PAST

AURORA'S DRESS WAS PINK. JUST LIKE THE DISNEY princess she was named for. Bryan's tie matched her dress. Bryan's eyes followed her everywhere. Bryan's mouth was all over her.

I shifted in my seat, taking in the room.

My friends were dancing with their dates. I was currently alone. Wallowing, unsure of why I came.

Bryan fucked me over. Now I was here, with his brother. And it was Bryan's idea. And the more I thought about it I wondered if he just said it so he could take responsibility for picking my date. For saying he allowed it. That it wasn't something I just decided to do. He took from me. Too much.

The truth was, I was here because it was this or stay at home for my senior prom and have that memory etched into my brain forever. Or at least until I left. I counted down the days every morning when I woke up. Every night before I went to sleep I wrote stories. They were all interweaving. A catalog of small-town drama. I wanted to do something with my stories one day.

I would be escaping. I wouldn't have to see Bryan anymore, and I wouldn't have to ache like this. I could fall for someone new, and maybe, if I was lucky, I could feel what it's like to have someone want you back.

Not be a little secret. To be in a real relationship.

What would that be like?

My father said we make our fate. He said he believed God had a plan in our life, but it was up to us to put it in motion. He said I was going to find someone who was there when I felt like falling. Someone who would want to take my hand and give me what I needed when I felt too much. Someone to make me laugh when happiness died. Bryan never made me laugh.

I didn't have my father's faith, not in the all mighty, heaven above, and all that. But I was going to force myself to have the same faith in myself as he had in me until I believed it.

My eyes drifted to my wrist. To the pale yellow corsage there.

Ben had done so well. I really owed him a lot.

I was glad he wasn't hovering over me. He knew I was still heart-broken over his brother. I looked for him in the room and found him by the punch. He was reaching into his coat pocket, laughing with one of his friends. A guy named Chet who played ball with him. When I saw Ben bring his drink to his coat, pouring something from a flask into it, I groaned, pushing off my seat.

I walked over to the guys and smiled widely when they looked at me. "What are you doing?" I kept my teeth clenched, aware a chap-erone was in my eye line, just over my date's shoulder.

Chet bailed, leaving Ben with me. "Adding some fun to the night." Ben smiled. All braces and swagger. I didn't know how he did it.

Well, I didn't know how he did it with the girls who fell all over themselves for him. I could see the appeal but even though one year wasn't much, I couldn't find him attractive in that way.

I reached out then, surprising him, for his drink. Maybe he had the right idea. Whatever he put in wasn't too strong. I could barely tell as it slid down my throat.

"What do you say?" Ben smiled, taking his empty glass from me.

"What?"

"Let's get drunk."

I smiled, my head feeling fuzzy. Okay, maybe that drink was stronger than it tasted. I had only had alcohol one other time in my life. I was a lightweight. Perhaps this was what I needed to get over the fact that Bryan and Aurora were walking around like it was their honeymoon.

"Let's stay and see who wins prom king and queen," I argued.

"Okay," Ben replied, taking my hand. It was the first time he had done that. I let him lead me out to the floor. He grabbed my other hand when we reached the center of the floor. He pulled my arms up and I interlaced my fingers behind his neck.

His hands went to my hips and I shivered. I had a low-backed dress. His fingertips touched me there and I pretended I hadn't felt it.

"It'll never work with him. You know that, right?" Ben said, into my hair.

"Nothing is happening anymore. I mean, I know. But how about you tell me why. Slip the knife in a little deeper."

"He will never leave her. Or this town."

"He will never leave Burlingame?"

"Nope."

"He doesn't like this town any more than I do." I recalled our conversations about the future. I was so vocal about leaving. He wasn't. He went back and forth. He could never pick a path. Time was running out.

"He says that. And maybe he doesn't, but he won't leave. The summer before my freshman year I always talked about leaving. I was obsessed with the travel channel that summer. And sometimes he told me I was stupid, or asked me why I would want to go. There are leavers, and there are those who grow roots. You and me? We are leavers. We don't belong here. He does, whether he wants to admit it or not. And maybe part of the reason he thinks he wants to leave is that he knows I will. And he knows you want to. So he thinks maybe he can have that, too. But the truth is the person he loves most is here. So he grows roots."

"Aurora," I pouted.

"My mother. And my mother wants Bryan and Aurora together more than anything in the world. For as long as I've been alive, it feels like, they've been this thing. She's like a sister to me. She is. And I know you have a certain perception of her. But you don't know her like I do. Like he does. Like my parents do. Because my family is her family."

"I'm not going to cry tonight." I said it out loud. I wanted to make it real.

"Then don't. Let's get out of here."

I looked around for Britt. Instead, I found Christina, huddled in a corner with the last person in the world I ever thought I would see her with. Rodney. I blinked, then shook my head. When I was sure I wasn't imagining things I looked up at Ben. "Neither one of us has a car."

"Well, that works perfectly with our plan then, huh?"

————

Ben and I snuck out of prom. My father wasn't home. He was staying with his sister for the night and the plan was for me to stay at Akia's with my friends. She lived out of town in a two-story farmhouse. I didn't even tell my friends I was leaving with Ben. I just did it. He had snuck me another drink while we were dancing and that was all the convincing I needed to leave.

We ran across the street to my house where I changed clothes. He ditched his tux jacket and we took off to the center of town, where we hoped no one would find us. When the gazebo fell into my gaze I took off running, throwing my shoes in the air. I heard Ben chase after me and it made me laugh out loud and that startled me. I couldn't remember the last time I laughed like that and even though I knew it was mostly the alcohol, I didn't care.

I fell to the ground and pushed my back up to the railing surrounding the gazebo. My cheeks were hot and my forehead felt slick.

"Has it ever happened to you?" I asked Ben. It took me a minute to realize I wasn't being specific with my question. That I was all in my head. "Have you ever been cheated on?" I elaborated.

"Yeah. A few times."

"Did it change you?"

"No. But I wasn't in love with any of the girls who did it. I think I was halfway out of the relationship and they didn't know how to end it, so it gave us both an excuse."

Ben always had a girlfriend. I wondered if he knew what it was like to be single. He was the boy with a girl in love with him every year. Suddenly I was remembering so many little things about him. We never talked before, but it was such a small school. I knew more about him than I thought. "I can't imagine what it would feel like. To love someone and have them betray you in that way. So I'm this person, and I've had a part in it. And that makes me sick."

"We are teenagers, Severin."

I had never heard him say my name before. I looked up at him and saw that he had pushed the sleeves of his white T-shirt up. He had tan arms. "Does that make it okay?"

"I don't know. I guess. We're kids. We make mistakes and it isn't real. At least not for me. Maybe for them. For you. But all of this," he said, motioning. I didn't know if he meant the town or high school or all of it jumbled together. "It isn't that serious. I'm not that serious."

"I can see that now." I smiled.

"Listen, we have enough serious at home. So I'm not about to invite any of that into my life. Not like Bryan. I guess that's the benefit of being the youngest. I see all of his mistakes and I learn from it, without the pain. You can spend your whole life trying to change him, and it's just going to be a dripping faucet of disappointment."

"I don't have my whole life. I have the rest of the year. The summer here."

"It'll never work."

I nodded, agreeing, but not being able to say the words. It was over. I just wanted to say it to his face. I wanted to make sure he knew I knew.

I LIKE YOU

I WALK OVER TO THE SCHOOL. REPLAYING OUR TIME together in my mind, cursing myself for not seeing the signs.

I look at his truck. Sitting there, waiting for *"repairs"*.

You can turn a blind eye to anything, I suppose. Humans are so good at it. I liked having some semblance of control. Being in charge for once. I didn't stop to ask why I always had to pick him up. Why I was his chauffeur.

Burlingame is so cozy, so happy and small. The way he walked to the grocery store, the gas station for gum, it made me miss my years here.

When I step into the school, I close my eyes, listening for him. The familiar sound of a basketball pulls me to the right, to the gym.

It's become our place. The place he first kissed me.

How many nights does he drink there? Without me? Is that how he spent his time before I showed up? The mighty fall so swiftly, so sadly. I once thought he had everything I wanted in life. More friends than I could count on two hands. A beautiful two-story home. A full family.

It was all a lie.

And he keeps digging further into himself, into his mistakes. He burrows there.

When I find him, he is staring at the hoop. The thud thud thud of the basketball hides my approach. I slip my shoes off at the side of the court and walk to him slowly, wringing my hands.

I tap him on the shoulder once he is within reach. I'm pulled back to high school days. When I would want his attention. So shy around him then. So bold now, except in this moment.

He turns to me. His beautiful blue eyes are sad. They're always sad. My own flicker past him, to the case of beer by the far wall.

I should have known. I should have known that patterns repeat whether you want them to or not, sometimes.

"Hi," I offer meekly.

"Hi." He is tight-lipped. I sense an urgency in his body. He turns away, sinks the basket.

We watch it, linger a moment too long in unison, the net swaying.

When he turns again, he grabs my hand, intertwines his fingers with mine. When I was a teen, I would have lit on fire over a moment like this. Now, I just feel something grow in the pit of my stomach.

"What's up?" His tone is casual, contradicting his slow movements and intimate motions.

"Nothing. I just wanted to see you." This is not how I planned to start this conversation. I talked to myself the entire walk over.

Granted, it wasn't a long walk, but it was a convincing argument I had with myself. I told myself not to get lost in the blue. In the touch. In the scent and taste of him. I needed to know what the hell he was doing.

"You don't have nothing face."

I want to kiss him for not letting me out of my questioning. For not letting me let things lie. Because as much as I hate him in this moment, I still feel the pull. "Why don't you drive your truck?"

"It doesn't run."

"Tell me the real reason," I say, pulling my hand from his. He doesn't release it.

He wants this. It was in his reply; he wants me to push. He always wants me to push him for the truth in the lie.

Finally, he unwinds his hand from mine, lets it fall. It slaps my bare thigh and the sound surrounds us. "Who told you?"

"I know I don't have many friends here anymore, but you couldn't expect me never to find out. Did you think it would go down that way? Maybe since I'm not going to be around forever."

"I didn't want you to know. What's wrong with that?"

"Did you do it back then, too?" I can't say the words, but I don't have to. He knows what I'm talking about.

"No!"

I think of my classmates. Bragging about flying down the dirt roads of our county. Flying fast. We don't have curves in Kansas, so the only way to feel like you're doing something dangerous is to amp the speed.

I knew they were drinking back then and I didn't know if Bryan was lying now or not. He ran with the kids who broke the rules. He wasn't sitting on the sidelines shaking his finger just because he was the preacher's son. But maybe his loathing of his father pushed him to do the stupid shit they did.

"You could have hurt someone! You could have hurt yourself!" My voice is loud, and I do not care.

"Don't you think I know that?" He walks away, to the side of the court. He grabs an open beer, tips it back.

I laugh. "How did I not notice?"

"Maybe you didn't care."

"Are you drunk now?"

"I don't get drunk. I never get drunk."

"So that makes it okay, then, right? You live your life buzzed?"

"Beats the alternative."

"Here we are again. Poor, poor Bryan. Always hiding from his actions and the consequences. Always hiding from reality."

"Sometimes the picture doesn't fit the reality. I'm never going to fit into this pretty picture you have in your mind. I'm not the prince you thought I was."

I throw my hands up. This is never-ending. I want off the ride. "Just stop."

"Am I boring you? Am I being a cliché?"

"No. This is beyond that. I just, I want more for you. Don't be your father."

"I can never be my father. Because you know who he gets to be now? The caring, understanding father. The one helping his poor son, fallen from grace, as he recovers. He is the one praying for me. He is the one who can't believe I would let this happen, but he will help me find my way. I will never be him. I will never let my bullshit get to my daughter."

"She will feed off you. She is a child, but fuck, she isn't stupid. You were that small innocent sponge once, too, remember? Every bad vibe, every little bit of loathing you carry in your heart for this life you are living, she will soak up. She will feel like the blame, the reason. She will wonder what your life would have been like if she had never been born if you keep treating your time on this earth with her here, in this town, like a prison. You only have so many nights, so many weekends, so many summers with her before she isn't your little girl anymore. Before this time fades away and she is gone, living her own life. Making her own mistakes and making her own family. Give her the best one, build it from this broken moment and these broken years. Build it up so it is solid and sure, for her."

"You're right. I know."

"Then do it. Don't you see how lucky you are? I bet she looks at you like you're the goddamn sun. She runs around you. Revolves. You're so lucky. I can see it from my fucking porch when you two run around that lawn out there. You're so lucky," I repeat myself.

"I know I am."

"Act like it. Don't be boring. Take this boring life, on paper, and live it to the fullest. Jesus."

"I know!"

"You can be pissed at me all you want. If that's what you need to take away the self-loathing you have for yourself."

He laughs solemnly. "So this is you helping. Okay."

"Always. I like to think I've come to know you. In a way others can't. Or maybe that's just what I want to tell myself. But there is this part of me that believes you think you're not seen. Or you can only be seen when you choke on your words. When you wear some sort of suffering on the outside. That you can't be loved if you openly express joy. Maybe that's the only way you found love from your parents. I don't know if that's right. Or if it's just the story I've written for you in my mind, and due to my own imagination, I've inserted my own reality into yours. I've projected this onto you. Does it sound right? I'm rambling. I'm rambling the way I used to with you. When I never knew what to say. And I'm so fucking mad at you right now I think it's just better that I fucking ramble."

"I like it. It takes me back."

"Love isn't about power. It isn't about having the upper hand. It's about this gentle ease. You just feel it with some people."

"There is something good coming from this. So maybe I'm not sorry for it."

"And what is that?" The anger comes again. I know he is sorry, but I hate his words.

"My mother has some peace because her son is a fuck-up. She gets out of that house. She gets her own office, helping with the real estate. I've never seen her like that. She is happy. She is helping me, because she truly loves me. And it's her escape. There it is. The thing you always want me to look for." He finishes his beer and I want to slap the empty can from his hand.

"There what is?"

"The silver lining."

My voice is a whisper. "It's always there, Bryan."

"So who told you? Ben?"

"Aurora."

"You talked to her?"

"She found me." I think back to high school. The scary meeting on the bench. The way I shivered in her presence. "She wanted to know what was going on with us. She wanted to make sure I would stay away from you."

"And is it going to work?"

"Yes." There is no doubt in my mind that this is over. I knew it once she told me.

"Wow. She's so good at what she does."

"If there's one thing I know, it's this: No one will care about your sadness as much as you do. No one will be as invested in it, fall apart for it, crumble with it. We all have our demons, and we will find people willing to hold our hands and help us, but no one can fight our battles for us. You need to figure out how you're going to overcome this." I walk past him, grab one of his beers.

"And by this, you mean my marriage?"

"Your sadness. It's deeper than you think, I believe."

"Say it."

"Depression?" I don't want to diagnose him. But I want to open the dialogue.

He barely lets me finish. "No. That's not it."

"Don't be like the rest of this town. Hiding from the real world and all there is out there. Thinking what we see on TV is make-believe."

"You're so supportive." His sarcasm is thick.

"I am. You may not see it right this second, because I have always been blunt. But maybe one day you'll look back on this moment and see it for what it was. Me, trying to help."

"And maybe I don't want any help." His words sound hollow. We both know he doesn't mean them.

"Oh, I'm aware." I humor him. "I've watched you double down on your walls. Your excuses. Your reasons for the isolation and the pity. It hate this, I hate *you* right now, Bryan. That's me being blunt. I want you to surprise me with your fight."

"You've always been the one with the words. They hurt, you know? They hurt, the way you use them. With the truth you throw around. Maybe some people don't want to deal with it. Yet. Just not yet."

"It's always going to be there like a ghost in the hallway."

"I'll never be like him, you know?"

I wonder if he is denying the similarities between him and his father again. We stare into each other's eyes and I see it. No. Not his father. "Ben? Not this again."

"Yes. This again. It's always going to be there."

"Well, it's a good thing this is done and I can do whatever I want."

"Was it one of those things where I was just something on your list? Something to check off? Gotta fuck the high school crush so I can tell all of my friends?"

"Speaking of your brother, he is never this immature." Well, he was. But not in this way. Not in the form of his emotions. He was surprisingly self-aware. It was too much at times. I wanted to be in a room with him. Not here. Building up, boiling over. I walk out of the gym, into the hallway, away from him.

I feel the fresh air of the night hit my face and listen for his next footsteps. At first, they don't come, and I get halfway down the lawn. Thinking I'm free. But soon I hear the echo of bare feet on concrete.

"And this is why we would never work, even if you stayed."

I turn around, face him. "Oh, do tell. Because I have a list a mile long of all the reasons why we would not work. But I'm curious about this one."

"Because you just say shit, and don't even try to filter out what will hurt someone."

"I let myself be this silent child in school. I was so scared of the popular kids and the real world and everything. Because I didn't have my mother to teach me how to be both strong and soft. So I just became a barbed wire. This has always been my defense, but you just didn't know me back then. Don't tell me something is new about me when you didn't even know me back then. You were too scared to let yourself. You were too scared to face the judgment of friends you probably don't even talk to anymore. No, I don't filter what I say. I'm sorry that hurts you but actions hurt more than words. You try to be this stoic guy, and maybe you think it's sexy, and maybe it *was* back then, but it's the way you treat people that will be remembered. Remember that."

I can see my front porch. It's so close, but I don't move. I don't want to be there. I don't know where I wish to be. Anywhere but Kansas.

I want to be anywhere but here with this mess that we've made. I don't know who I am anymore, and the more I examine my past transgressions, and what I've let my body do here in the present, the more I'm not sure of where I'm trying to get to.

I want to be easy, find who I'm meant to be with, without hurting others.

It's strange, the way I am drawn to Ben. His brother's body fits into mine so easily, so smoothly. But it isn't what I hoped for. It wasn't something to check off a list. It wasn't something I ever thought would happen and I don't feel fuller for it.

I feel weighed down by my own duality.

"Don't go," he says, reading my mind. Sensing my splitting apart. I don't want it to be alone. And I hate myself a little for that. The days are winding down and the hole in my heart, left by my father, needs to be filled somehow, some way. "I just want it to be easy again," he whispers.

"It's never been easy. We've just pretended it was," I reply.

"Pretending is fun sometimes, right? Can we pretend again?" Bryan asks. And it would be so easy to fall into him. But my body recoils.

"I want to," I admit.

"Maybe you were right. We were never meant to be anything permanent."

"I like you." My voice is unsteady, and he mistakes it for weakness. He reaches for me and this is when I break. I pull my hand away, not letting him touch me. "I love her." My voice cracks as I think of my friend. "I loved her. I loved her and she was taken from me. From her family. From her friends and this town. This world is smaller without her and her friendship. There is someone out there who was meant to love her and maybe they never met her and they felt the loss when she closed her eyes. I believe in stuff like that. Romance and tragedy and the way we carry that. She was taken from this world because someone was stupid and selfish and you know that. You've seen the way it can rip a community apart. The way it can rip someone apart. Do you know how long it took me to recover from that? I had to leave here. I had to hide in a city full of millions. And I cried myself to sleep every night. I had to be put back together. I wrote stories for her, because she, above all else, encouraged me. She never got to read them. She never got to go out and conquer the world. And she would have. How dare you be that selfish. How dare you be that stupid. You can't love someone you don't respect. And I have none for you now. I can barely look at you."

"How could you not see it before? Did you really think this dark pit I fell into was just because of Aurora? It's because I've been hating myself. I hate myself. Is that not enough?"

"No. You're going to take mine, too. And Aurora? She loves you. She loves you. The good and the bad and all of it. Just go. Go back to her and stop this endless bullshit. I'm done. I'll be gone soon."

"You're so good at running."

"Don't confuse this with running," I argue. "I'm just done with things that do not serve me. And you are one of those things. You always have been." The truth hurts, and I've been hiding from this truth for too long.

His voice cracks, and I hurt for the boy I thought I loved when he looks at me. "Goodbye shouldn't sound like this."

"Should it sound like last time? Where I don't even give you one?"

"Maybe this time I would have preferred that."

"I guess I don't care anymore. To give you what you want. To serve myself on a platter for you. Maybe this is growth. Maybe you should study it."

"I am. I'm always studying you."

"If you were, you would have known to be there when I needed you. My father is dead. I lost him. And the person there for me, was Ben."

THUNDERING

PAST

THE HEAT OF THE NIGHT WRAPPED AROUND ME AS I heard the rapping on my door. A heavy hand and my heart was suddenly so very heavy. I threw the covers off, ran to my door. My father never came in unless I said I was awake or opened the door. He allowed me my sanctuaries, wherever I could find them.

I opened the door to his long face, his red eyes. "Can you come into the kitchen, dear?" His voice was a tremor and I started to shake. My mind raced to my sister, so many miles away, in a city that terrified me.

I followed him to the kitchen. The light over the stove was on, casting a yellow glow around us. My father was wearing the blue and white striped pajamas my sister sent last Christmas. A gift from us both. She always described the gifts to me on the phone, then wrote my name on the card.

My father pulled out a seat, so I took it. The wood made loud bumbling sounds as I pulled it back in. "What's going on?" My voice was a whisper, hollow. "Is it Aunt V?"

"No," my father replied, calming my heart a moment. "And it's not your sister." He quieted it even more.

"Then what?"

"There's been an accident." My ears rang. My heart raced wilder, more thundering. I thought of Britt. My lone friend with a car.

"Is it Brittany?" My father shook his head, reached for my hand. I let him take it. I wanted answers, but I would take this comfort to get me through the next seconds.

"It's Christina." My breath left me, and my father's voice became a buzzing noise. "She was in a car accident."

"She doesn't have a car," I replied. Disbelieving.

"I know. But she was in an accident. She was the passenger."

"Is she okay?" I knew the answer. It was just what you said when you heard news like this. You had hope in your chest and you needed to let it out before it was curb stomped on the ground. My father's head went back and forth, swaying. Or maybe I was swaying in my seat. I stood up, my chair flying back, hitting the wall behind me. "FUCK!" I screamed. My father stood, gathering me in an instant.

There was too much death. Too many years stood between this one and the last, but it still felt raw. My heart was crumbling, the air in the room was being swallowed by my heavy gasps. I slid slowly to the floor, pulling from my father. My hands wrapped around my knees and I wept. There was silence around me, my cries cut through it.

The phone rang on the wall. The old one my father would never replace with a cordless. He picked it up and I choked on my heaving, wanting to hear every word he said.

"Yes. She knows. I'm with her. Okay, okay. Yes. Yes, in the morning." My father hung the phone up, stared at his feet.

"Who was that?" my voice cracked, ragged and red.

"The Winthrop boy." I couldn't be sure which one would be calling. It was tangled now. My brief evening with Ben, where I was sullen and confused, then laughing, meant we were tied in some way. He smiled at me in the hallways now, and I felt like I had a new friend. Someone else on my side. "I told him you would talk to him in the morning."

I wouldn't be talking to anyone in the morning that wasn't my father, my sister, Britt, or Akia.

My father moved around me. Opening kitchen doors. Opening the fridge. He let me sit in my bubble, never intruding.

I smelled oatmeal, honey, and lavender when he washed his hands. I heard my cell phone, emergency only, going off in my bedroom. This was an emergency, right? Except, there was nothing anyone could do. My best friend. The other one of us who was ready to float out of this town, ready to take the world and make it hers. The one of us who had no fear. No quavering voice. She had the steady hand and someone had stilled it. I smelled oatmeal, horror.

I grabbed the chair next to me, pulled myself up. I laid my forehead on the seat, half anchored, half trying to be vertical.

"You don't have to eat it," my father said. "It's just habit. I didn't know what to do." He knew what to do. It was in his presence. Just being there. I wouldn't be eating what he made but it felt good to put my hands around the bowl. To let the steam touch my face. My father went to the couch, turned on the lamp. He sat down and watched me. I wasn't sure what he was looking for, what he was waiting for me to do. I was numb and movement seemed hard.

"I think I just want to go back to bed." The words came out, autopilot. "I think I need to...be alone." I wouldn't say I needed to sleep. That was a lie. I looked at the clock on the wall. Three a.m. I sometimes woke at that hour. I would stare out my window at the school, count how many hours of sleep I was missing. Try to weigh and measure how tired I would be.

———

I never made it to my graduation. I had one week of solitude ahead of me before the day was to come. We had plans. So many plans. Britt was taking us to Topeka. We were searching for the perfect outfit to wear under our gowns. We were going to meet at my house to decorate our caps. We were getting manicures and pedicures. We were ready to walk down that aisle. Say goodbye to Burlingame. Steps into the future.

Instead, I stayed in bed for two days, until Tuesday. I only took calls from my sister, Akia, and Britt. I called neither of the Winthrop boys back. I had no intention of calling any of the Winthrop boys back.

Christina was in the car with someone from school. Someone who had been drinking. Christina did not drink. She also did not, to our knowledge, spend time with the person who was the reason she would never see her high school graduation. She had never, to our knowledge, shared a friendship or her desired romance, with Rodney. They'd known each other since kindergarten, just like the rest of us. But they did not speak. They did not.

Except they must have. They must have known each other in a way the rest of us did not know. They told us he was taking her home.

This would have been the time we investigated. The time for us to tear everything apart. To look for the clues. To form an alliance. To create a plan. But the plans were done. We would never scheme again.

Our past was worth saving. I wanted to place it in a jar, carry it with me. I wanted to pull it out when I left. Press it against my cold window. Instead, I buried it all. I pushed it into the caverns of my heart. I pushed it there to rest with my mother. I wanted to run away and nothing felt right except the possibility of escape.

I made a list for my father. He taught me that. When I wanted something irrational, something crazy, to write it down. I could examine my choice that way. I could determine if it was too outlandish. I could possibly talk myself out of my crazy desire. It normally worked. This time it did not. I wanted to leave Burlingame that week. I was a high school graduate. No ceremony was necessary. It was a formality I no longer cared for. I could not walk into that building again and not see my friend. I could not see the faces of my other friends. It would be too much.

I planned to beg, if the list didn't work. But it never came to that. My father agreed to cut our summer short. He agreed to change my plane ticket. I would be going to live with my sister within a week. When I broke the news to Akia and Britt, they admitted they had no intention of going to graduation either, but their parents thought it would be good for them. I thanked God for my father then. There were times when he made me do something I didn't want to do, arguing I would regret it. And he was always right. But he did not argue me on this. He saw into my wounded heart. He saw into my red eyes, and he knew.

There was nothing left to do here. There was nothing left to see and I could not live in a prison of memories again. I needed to write away my grief in a new place. In any way I wished. I needed to pretend shame couldn't catch me.

I never told my friends I wouldn't be going to Christina's funeral.

GRIEF ALONE

TWO WEEKS PASS. A FLURRY OF PLANS AND ENDS BEING tied. My sister and aunt take over. Fuss and fold into each other. They laugh, telling stories, and I sit at the kitchen table, absorbing them.

When they are gone, I pack things at the house. Take pictures off the wall. On a Saturday, I pull an old black dress from my closet for the funeral. I hold their hands when they lower my father into the ground. I catch Ben's eyes from across the cemetery.

He is this strange mixture of wild and steady—sneaking into my window at night, holding me close to him. I touch him everywhere, seeking comfort in him, but he is steady. He never gives in to the want I pour on him that we both know is wrapped in grief. He gives me what I need. He gives me laughter and steadiness. He gives me his ear and his mouth close, telling me his secrets—the way he pined for me as a teenager, the things I never saw. I fall into him every night he is close, and it scares me.

During the day, I busy myself. We get ahold of the *other* town realtor. The house goes on the market and I leave the sheet I tacked up over my window up. I keep the sunlight out and I keep Bryan out. I block his number, not out of hatred, but out of necessity.

When my sister brings in a picture taken from prom night, this is when the tears come and fall more freely. When the dam breaks and I realize the well inside me was not dry.

I look at our faces. Me and Britt and Akia and Christina.

"You never talk about her anymore," Sasha says.

"I felt her inside for so long, and then I pushed it down. Coming here, it was too much. It's so hard, all this losing."

"I know," she says, looking away, to a picture of our mother on the wall. I hug my sister then. I don't let her hug me, I hug her. I try to comfort her. I try to be the one giving, not the one taking. My sponge sister and all of her worry.

"I love you so much. Thank you for raising me. I'm sorry I didn't turn out quite right."

She laughs. "You turned out perfect." When she pulls away she wipes at my cheek.

"When are you leaving?" I ask her. She has been packing her things, slowly. I hear her talking to my aunt about money. She can't stay here forever. And my aunt can tie up the loose ends. She was left in charge of my father's estate.

"On Monday, maybe. What are your plans?"

It's a Tuesday and next Monday seems so far away and too soon. Six days left with my sister. "I don't know. Maybe I should leave at the same time."

"There isn't any reason to stay. Unless you want to spend more time with Aunt V."

I think of my aunt and her life in Topeka. She doesn't spend nights here and I don't want to be alone in this house. "I don't want to be here, by myself," I say, voicing my own sad thoughts.

"Would you be alone?" She eyes me and I shake my head. "I know he comes over. It's okay. You could have had him come through the door. You're not a kid and I'm not your mom."

"I'll remember that the next time you give me the mom look."

She laughs, walking from my bedroom. I follow her and pull my phone out. I see a text from Ben and I miss him even though I saw him this morning. I also see a text from Britt. I smile, then show my sister.

"You can't carry grief alone. You can't run from the ones you love, you know." She hands my phone back and I shove it in my pocket.

"I know." I look at the kitchen table. At the rest of the pictures my sister has been sorting. Prom pictures. The ones I left behind, shoved in the hall closet. I grab another one from the table. I see Christina, our Prom Queen. I see her in her crown. Her blue dress. An image that I can only see here, never pull from my memory. Because I left prom early. I didn't see her win, because I didn't want to see Bryan win prom king, which he did. I didn't see Rodney congratulate her, ask her to dance. I didn't see the beginning of the end. The beginning of fate's cruel trick.

I run my finger over the gold and glimmer of her crown.

You can't run from your past forever. You can't avoid the grief in your chest. It will lie dormant, but eventually bubble up and over, overtaking you.

I pull my phone back out, and send a text.

———

Britt meets me at the cemetery. She is already standing at Christina's grave, a place I never let myself go. A place I could not face.

When I reach her, I reach for her hand. She lets me take it and I begin to cry. Maybe I don't deserve forgiveness, but she is giving me this.

She turns to me when a sob escapes, and hugs me. She feels the way she always did. A little taller than me. Her chin rests on the top of my head and I know her neck will be covered in my salt. Christina was my best friend. I always told myself that. But Britt was the one who always challenged me. She was the one who always told me the truths I didn't want to face.

"I'm so sorry," I sob. "I shouldn't have left like that. I should have kept in touch and you would think, with all this death, I would be better at this. But I'm not. Maybe they coddled me too much." My father who is gone and my sister who will be gone soon, too. Will I always be so stunted?

"It's okay," Britt says, pulling away. "I'm sorry about your father. And I'm sorry things were shit when we saw each other again." She turns away, looks at Christina's grave. I let my eyes follow. Christina Kaylen. Daughter. Granddaughter. Friend.

I lay my head on Britt's shoulder and listen to the silence of Kansas. My breathing becomes even and I know I cannot stay in this silence. "I'm leaving soon," I say. "I couldn't bail again without telling you."

"How soon?"

"Next week. Same day as my sister. The house is almost taken care of and we need to get back to the lives on pause." She nods and we stand in silence again.

"Who do you think she would have been?" I ask.

"I don't know. I think she would have been a vet. Or a foster parent. Or a journalist. Anything. I don't know," she repeats. "She wanted to be so many things. And now she is none of those." She shuffles her shoe and I close my eyes.

I open them when a bird cries and I look at the words on the tombstone. "She was our friend. She will always be our friend. That can't be taken away."

"Yes. Maybe you're right." Britt clears her throat. "I have a question though."

I take my head from her shoulder, look her in the eye. "Yes?"

"Is your friendship still going to be something that was taken from me that night?"

I press my lips together and I hate this feeling in my throat. Tears keep coming out of me and it's a foreign thing. I was always so good at numbing, running. "No," I say. We don't hug again. We just nod. Letting the knowledge sink in that beginnings can belong to those who never had proper endings.

We stay there in the cemetery until our stomachs rumble and the heat is too much, then head to lunch. Together.

I LOVE HER

I'm taking a break from packing my car, scolding Beau for jumping in the front seat, when Ben finds me. He has roses. He has my heart in knots.

He grabs one of my suitcases from the lawn, asks me where it needs to go, as I busy myself with the open trunk, the overflowing going on there.

When he finally looks at me, his arms are crossed over his chest, and I'm blushing, wondering if he thinks I'm leaving him again. Without a goodbye. The roses are now on my hood, pulling at my eyes.

"Yes?" I say, shaking my head.

"Where are you going, Sev?"

"I don't know," I reply. And it's not a lie. I could drive home to California. I could drive to New York to spend some time with my sister. I'm thinking about flipping a coin. Ben and I haven't discussed whatever is going on with us. My life has been too heavy, with no moment to discuss relationships and feelings that aren't grief.

"Where do you want to go, Sev?"

"I don't know," I repeat. Ben takes a seat in the grass, and I walk over to him. I place my knees on the grass, too, one on each side of him, caging him. He lets his hands wander down my back, pulling me closer. I don't care who sees me straddling him on the lawn. I just want to be close to him one more time. Before we have to address this or undress this.

I place my hands on his cheeks, and he looks back, into my eyes. For once, not brimming with salt. "I've been crying too much, Ben. I'm so tired of it."

"I know." He kisses my jaw, and this feels natural. It doesn't ache, not in the way I have craved. I craved pain and love. I mixed it all up, convinced myself they had to be intertwined. Ben makes me feel like myself. The me that is buried under the sarcasm and the things I run from.

"When are you leaving?" I ask.

"Whenever you do," he says, echoing earlier words. I bite his neck in response. He laughs. "I'm serious. There's nothing essential for me here. My mother is doing better than she ever has, and I think she may leave my father. And Bryan. That's never going to be some sitcom bullshit brotherly love thing. It's just you here that I find...worth it."

I pull him close, close my eyes, then open them. I stare across the lawn, and it's so sunny out. So bright and I know he will go have lunch with me if I ask him. He will go have dinner with me if I ask him. He will walk around with my hand in his, in front of everyone. He will let the sun hit his face as he kisses me, never hiding.

I pull away, untangle myself from him and the ground. I walk to my car without a word and sit in the driver's seat. I leave the door open, and Ben gets up, coming to me. He kneels on the pavement of the driveway and places one arm on the side of my seat, the other shoots out, grabbing my hand on the steering wheel.

"Let's leave town together," he says, soft.

I shake my head. I can't do it. But fuck, I want to. I want to fall for this man, but I'm terrified. I'm terrified of what genuine love looks like. I'm terrified of all-consuming.

"No," I say, a tear running down my cheek.

"Why?" he asks. "Why can't you let yourself have this? What have we been doing? I'm here every night. And you let me hold you, and you let me kiss you, and it feels different, right? You're not still thinking about him, are you?"

I look at him, startled. I see it in his face then. The doubt. In these short weeks, I have felt more for him than I ever felt for Bryan. It's real, what I feel. It doesn't hurt, and it isn't some fantasy-chasing game. He is my friend, and I know I could fall for him. I know I could have more with him than I have ever had with anyone. "No. God, no," I say, flipping my hand over, taking his.

"Then what is it?"

"What is it you want? I live in LA, and you live, where? I don't even know where you live."

"I told you. Connecticut," he answers, laughing at us.

"Okay, where are we going to run away to?"

"Wherever we want," he replies.

I pull my hand away, let it fall to the bottom of the steering wheel. "No," I say, again.

"Why, Severin?"

I look away from my hands then, pulling the visor down, pretending to look for something in my eyes. There's nothing in my eyes but my sadness. He repeats his question, and I close my eyes, giving him a piece of the truth. "Because...I like you," I whisper.

"And?"

"I love her," I reply, looking into my own eyes. I wait a moment, then break my own stare, and look at him. I see he gets it. I see he knows.

He stands and clears his throat. "C'mere," he says, reaching for me. I take his hand and get out of the car. I lean back against it, looking up into his eyes. "You make love a tragedy. You have. But you and I, we don't have to. This is what I want. I want to drive back home. And I want you to come with me. I have one month left of this summer, and I know you want to spend some more time with your sister, and she is a hop, skip, and a jump away from me. So we can get in my car, and we can take that ride, and we can forget all of this, and we can laugh, and we can unburden ourselves. We can have sex in hotels, and we can take wrong turns, and you do not have to lose yourself, and stop loving yourself, to like me. Those two things do not go hand in hand. And when we are done with this trip, you can fly back here and get your car and go back to your life. Unburdened. You can do whatever you want. I'm not here to weigh you down. I'm here to make you laugh and to make you smile, but never forget the things you want to hold onto."

I'm crying, and it feels so strange to cry this way. Tears of hysteria and confusion over his words. Because I know he could be all-consuming and I know he would heal me. I shake my head and he smiles at me.

"What are you feeling?" He laughs.

"I thought you said you could read me?" I dare, and he runs his hand through his hair, looking beautiful and steady, like a second chance. I walk to him, stopping his hand, running a thumb over his jaw before he can answer. "Them good moth flutters. I'm feeling them good moth flutters, Ben."

EPILOGUE

BEN

YOU CAN LEARN A LOT ABOUT A WOMAN DURING A CAR ride from Kansas to New York City. You can also learn a lot about a dog during a car ride of that length.

Spoiler alert: His asshole reeks.

Severin—the girl I've wanted since I saw her in a pale yellow dress the night of her senior (and my junior) prom—agreed to drive home with me to Connecticut. We made a detour to New York City so she could see her sister, but Severin and her dog—Beau—came home with me for a few weeks.

It didn't make a lick of sense on paper, and she had *just* answered the big question of whether or not her childhood crush on my older brother was worth it.

Another spoiler alert for you: I always knew it wasn't, and I was proven correct.

Goddamn, I love to be right.

And, by the way, when she laughs at me, I don't think that snarky heart in her chest is bruised much.

Do I hate my brother the way Severin assumed? No. He's just not the first person I'd call if I got mugged—or got my heart broken.

You can't fix "jackass"—and unfortunately, my brother and I were both born with different strains of it.

Anyway, enough about that buzzkill.

Severin had spent a few weeks with me before flying back to Kansas, leaving Beau with me for the time being. She picked her car up in Burlingame and then drove it the long way back to LA.

And this is where things get exciting, my friends.

My girl—I can call her that now—packed up her belongings, and she is driving to me, to *us*, right now.

I don't have much. A small apartment with a few pictures on the wall and a big window that overlooks the *luxurious* parking lot.

Beau and I are sitting backward on the couch, overlooking said parking lot. I have my chin in my hands, and I keep checking my phone, doing the math in my head after checking her last text.

I look at Beau, then at the yellow roses on the console table by the door. "Yeah, boy. Any minute now."

He cocks his head at me like he doesn't believe me, and somehow, like he thinks my choice in roses is dumb.

Yes, yellow symbolizes friendship, but Severin's my best friend. And back in Kansas, as we waded in the water, she told me I was her *only* friend there.

If she decides to live with me here, I'll be her only friend again until she makes my home her home.

I hope this isn't just wishful thinking.

Beau groans, like he can read my mind. I think he's really sick of my shit, and I can't say I blame him. I'm sick of my Severin-is-gone moping, too.

I'm in love with a girl who should have been mine ten years ago, but you can't waste time crying over spilled milk or lost years.

So, when she walks in that door, I'm going to tell her I love her.

I'm staring at Beau, having a silent argument about miles per hour and the average length of Severin's rest breaks—something we both know are lengthy—when she pulls up.

The shape of her little Volkswagen Beetle is unmistakable to both of us. My eyes go wide, and Beau starts barking a little too loudly.

"Shush it, mister," I scold with a laugh, looking for his leash. I slip my Vans on, leash the beast, grab the roses, and then open the door.

We bound down the stairs, and when I hit the bottom one, Beau takes off running. I kind of like my arm, and I know Severin does too; so in the interest of keeping my right one, I let the leash go and let the brute run to his mother.

Severin cries out as her four-legged boy reaches her, nearly knocking her over.

"Shit, sorry!" I holler, jogging to them. I step on his leash so he can't take off, giving him the stink eye as I do it.

Severin looks exactly like I imagined she would after a drive across the country—like home, like everything my teenage hormones wanted, and everything my grown ass can't live without.

She smiles at the roses, shaking her head. I set them on the hood, then wrap my arms around her, breathing in the scent of her hair when her head hits my chest. She mumbles against me.

"What's that, Sevvy?"

She laughs, pinching my side. "I can *feel* your feelings rolling off you like waves."

"Oh yeah?" I grab her hand, pulling her wrist up to my mouth. My favorite things about this woman are her mouth, her wit, her fight, and the dark ass memes she sends me. I missed everything about her while she was gone, and already, I don't want her to leave.

She said she would go home, pack up her life in California, and drive back to me. And when she returned, she would have an answer— New York City with her sister, or Connecticut with me.

My offer isn't as shiny as the one her sister has for her.

But I have that look she is giving me right now. I have the knowledge that I make her give me that look.

"What am I feeling then, Severin?"

"Happiness. Doubts." She smirks, pressing into me. "*Want.*"

I could fall into that, but I don't. "Yeah, more on the *'want'* later, lady. I'm going to do several questionable things to that ass once we get inside. Back to the doubts."

Is that my heart thundering in my chest? Fuck.

She rolls her eyes. "Let me wash the car ride off first." And then, "Okay, yes, doubts."

I lean back, onto her car, giving Beau a nod since he's decided *now* is the time to sit still and listen. *Sure as shit is.* "Since you can feel my doubts so well, Severin Thompson, if I were to ask you one question right now, what do you think it would be?"

She leans on the car, right next to me, her finger grazing the top of my sweatpants. "What did I unburden myself of while I was gone?"

Yeah, that's my heart thundering.

I checked the weather earlier—blue skies for miles "And?" I ask.

She steps around me, settling between my legs, gripping the front of my white T-shirt. "I would tell you, clothes. Expectations. Hereditary traits. Dreams. Lies. A false *home*."

I hold my finger up to indicate that I need a minute, then I grab her hips, pushing her back a bit. I grab Beau's leash and open her car door, securing it in the door when I shut it.

Big ass farting bastard isn't going anywhere or interrupting me when I ask her to clarify.

This is kind of a big deal in my world.

I grab Severin again, and this time she yelps, legs wrapping around my waist as I bring her to the rear of the car, pressing her against the back of it. "False home? What's that?"

She brings her lips to my neck, kissing me, her fingers tangling in my shoulder-length hair.

She likes it long, and I'm never cutting it again.

"Anywhere that brings me away from you. That's a false home," she clarifies. "You know I love you, right?"

I still, letting her slide down the back of her car until her feet intentionally land on my shoes. Her chin tips up, and I bring my thumb to her bottom lip.

Did I know that?

I hoped for it. I sure as shit hoped.

The sun is setting, and the pinks and reds of her cheeks bring me back. The grin that takes over my face can only be described as evil. *This echoes her past words, not mine.*

"What?" she asks, slapping my chest.

"You really are a watercolor, Severin Thompson."

She smacks me again. "I just drove across the country to tell you *I love you*, Ben Winthrop. What the hell do you have to say for yourself?"

I wink. "I like you."

"Fuck off."

She moves to go around me, and I grab her by the hip, pressing my mouth to her ear. *"And* I love you. And do you know how it feels?"

She leans into me, two tiny fists in my shirt again, mouth over my heart. "How?"

"All-consuming."

Her arms go around my waist when I say those words—and I know it's the way she wants to be loved. It's the way I freely love her.

I press a kiss to her forehead, then grab her hand. Turning, I say, "Now grab that stinky ass dog of ours and let's get up upstairs, babe. Let's go home."

———

Keep reading for a preview of I Love You, I Need Him.

ACKNOWLEDGMENTS

As always, thank you to my family and friends. This career has been a ride, and I appreciate your encouragement and patience.

Thank you to all of the bloggers. You are rock stars.

Talon, thank you for being a kickass beta and encourager. I was so lost with this book until you read it.

Kathy, thank you for loving this story. I can't wait to read yours.

Cynthia, girl I am so glad I found you! I feel like I found my writing twin. Keep telling your truths. It gives me the courage to keep telling mine.

My Rebels, YOU ALL ROCK! Thank you for making me laugh and for sharing your lives with me.

Kat, thank you for everything you do. Thank you for being my travel buddy and the one who drives me through the night halfway across the country.

Christina, thank you for the insanity. I could not do any of this without your devotion. You want nothing but good for me. And that's all I want for you and your crazy stories. I can't wait to hug you.

And lastly, thank you to my readers. I get to do this because of you.

J.R. Rogue first put pen to paper at the age of fifteen after developing an unrequited high school crush & has never stopped writing about heartache. She has published multiple volumes of poetry and novels.

Three of her poetry collections, La Douleur Exquise, Exits, Desires, & Slow Fires, & I'm Not Your Paper Princess have been Goodreads Choice Awards Nominees.

She is a 200hr Certified Yoga Teacher, with additional certification in Yoga Nidra and Trauma-Informed Yoga.

She lives in a small town in the midwest with her family.

To keep up with everything she's working on join her facebook group, Rogue's Rebels.

www.jrrogue.com
contact@jrrogue.com

- facebook.com/jrrogueauthor
- twitter.com/jenr501
- instagram.com/j.r.rogue
- amazon.com/J.-R.-Rogue
- bookbub.com/authors/j-r-rogue
- pinterest.com/rogueauthor
- snapchat.com/add/jenr501

ALSO BY J. R. ROGUE

NOVELS

MUSE & MUSIC SERIES

Breaking Mercy

Burning Muses

Background Music

Blind Melody

SOMETHING LIKE LOVE SERIES

I Like You, I Love Her

I Love You, I Need Him

I Like You, I Hate Her

RED NOTE SERIES

The Rebound

SUMMER OF SECRETS SERIES

Teach Me

STANDALONE NOVELS

Kiss Me Like You Mean It

POETRY

GOODREADS CHOICE AWARDS NOMINEES

La Douleur Exquise

Exits, Desires, & Slow Fires

I'm Not Your Paper Princess

Tell Me Where it Hurts

Rouge

An Open Suitcase & New Blue Tears

Le Chant Des Sirènes

Apus

Breakup Poems

I Have Sold a Beautiful Lie

Viral

This Witch

After The Blackout

LETTERS TO THE UNIVERSE

Poems for the Moon: Vol 1

Poems for the Moon: Vol 2

Poems for the Stars: Vol 1

Poems for the Stars: Vol 2

Poems for the Dawn: Vol 1

Poems for the Dawn: Vol 2

Made in United States
North Haven, CT
11 February 2022

15988927R00169